GETTING ALL RILED UP

ERIN NICHOLAS

ABOUT THE BOOK

Sex. God. Those are the words used to describe Derek Wright around Sapphire Falls.

But now that Derek wants to change his cocky ways and date nice-girl Lucy Geller, those words are coming back to bite him in the ass.

His best friend's little sister, Riley, isn't about to let Derek turn his attention on her sweet friend Lucy. He isn't good enough—and Riley has no trouble telling him that.

But when Derek asks for her help in reforming him from rouge to romantic, Riley can't resist the opportunity to mess with the irritating, know-it-all playboy a little. Because *she* is not a nice girl.

But she might just be the right girl for him...

This book was previously published as After Tonight.

ISBN: 978-0-9988947-1-3

Editors: Kelli Collins

Cover by Qamber Designs & Media

1

"Sex. God."

Riley Ames perked up at the two words from the blond at the next table. Who wouldn't? The other woman was talking to her friend, but that was eavesdrop-worthy stuff right there.

"The man should open a spa or a clinic or something."

"A sex spa?" her friend asked with a laugh.

"I'm not kidding," the first woman went on. "I have never felt as good as I did after that weekend with him. Relaxed, happy, beautiful, and completely spent. I smiled for days after that. And I didn't get my vibrator out for over two weeks. It was that good."

Okay, seriously? Riley was supposed to concentrate on her work with *that* conversation going on three feet away? She pivoted her computer and surreptitiously scooted her chair so that she could see the women better. She continued to study her laptop screen, pretending to be focused on her own work, but she was completely tuned in to the conversation now.

The blond was curvy and had half of the inventory at Sephora on her face. And, if she was from around here, then she'd gotten that Sephora online because there wasn't a store for fifty miles, Riley noted as an aside. One more strike against Sapphire Falls.

Riley was all about makeup and the fun that could be had with a good palette of colors and some high-quality brushes. She easily spent an hour getting ready every morning herself. But she didn't like to *look* like she spent an hour getting ready every morning. Less was more.

Sephora was the one who knew the Sex God. She was drinking red wine and wore a fitted black dress that was a little much for the Come Again, the only bar in Sapphire Falls. The dress code here went a little less lace and a lot more denim.

"And I didn't care about Zach *at all* after that weekend," she said. "I mean, this guy completely fucked him out of my system."

Well, okay then.

"You were almost *engaged* to Zach," her friend, a brunette with curls and more of a girl-next-door look, said.

"I know. That's what I'm saying. No more booty calls for Zach. No more letting him walk all over me. I'm cured."

Riley couldn't help but be a bit impressed with that. Sex God for the win.

It wasn't that she didn't realize how sad it was to be completely into this conversation and intrigued by another person's sex life. But she was in Sapphire Falls. Tiny, everything's-always-the-same, everyone-knows-everyone Sapphire Falls. And she'd now been here for three months. Creepy or not, listening to this woman talk about an amazing weekend of sex was the most interesting conversation she'd had in a while.

She was living in her parents' basement, sleeping 'til noon —or trying to at least, when her mom didn't bang around the house at the crack of dawn—wearing sweatpants all day, eating chips by the bagful, and on her computer until three a.m. every morning. And yes, she was online gaming for several of those hours. Because the work she was doing was easy and, frankly, there wasn't very much of it. Hence, the need to be living with her parents again at the age of twenty-six.

Basically, she had reverted back to her thirteen-year-old self. And her fourteen-year-old self. And fifteen. And...yeah, it was sad and pathetic. And she, unlike this very satisfied, over-her-ex woman, had *not* gone two weeks without her vibrator.

Okay, so *that* was a little different from her teenage self.

But otherwise, Riley was right back where she'd started—and she was about to go crazy.

Maybe she needed to meet this Sex God. She had to admit that she'd had some pretty good sex. She was no stranger to hot-sweaty-awesome weekends. But she wasn't sure she'd been with anyone she would label a God. And *definitely* not in Sapphire Falls.

"So you need this guy," Sephora said. "We'll chat with him tonight, and then you can come back here on Friday, okay?"

Riley perked up at that. The Sex God would be *here*? Oh yeah, this was getting all kinds of interesting. And she was very grateful to these two women. She might have to buy their next round.

Riley settled back in her chair and pulled up a game of solitaire. No way was she leaving before she saw the God for herself, and no way could she concentrate on the new website design she was doing now.

"I don't know," the brunette said. "I'm not very good at flirting and stuff."

Her friend laughed. "That's part of the beauty. You don't even have to be good at it. *He's* good at it."

"What's he look like?" Curly asked.

Yeah, what's he look like, Sephora? Riley asked in her head. She was beyond curious now.

"Tall, big hands." Sephora laughed. "He's got dark brown hair, gorgeous blue eyes and he's built. He does a bunch of manual labor—yard work, construction, farm work—so he's in great shape, has great abs, a fabulous ass, and *arms...*" She sighed happily.

Riley assumed she meant that he had great arm *muscles* because if he was doing yard work and farm work, having *arms* was pretty helpful, but she refrained from commenting. Or snorting out loud. She cracked herself up sometimes.

"Is he easy to talk to?" Curly asked, scratching at the label on her beer bottle.

Ah, she's a little nervous, Riley thought. So this one wasn't quite as into fucking her ex out of her system with a weekend fling, perhaps.

"He's a huge flirt," Sephora told her. "You won't have to worry much about talking. Except the dirty kind," she said with a grin. "He's really good at that."

Riley had to admit that dirty talk was a mark in the pro column for her too. But she wanted to know if the guy didn't *need* to talk much because women's panties just dropped off whenever he was around, or if he didn't have much to say that was interesting or noteworthy. As in, he mostly read *Sports Illustrated*, had all the ESPN channels on his cable package, and spent his time hunting and fishing with his buddies where quiet was a must.

And none of that narrowed down who this guy was.

Riley acknowledged that she was being super judgmental. Yes, the guys around here were interested in things she had no interest in. Yes, she had a hard time having an engaging conversation with most of them. But that didn't mean they weren't nice guys. They were, by and large. In fact, they were almost *too* nice. And hey, if the woman only needed Sex God for his magic cock, then it didn't really matter if he used his computer mostly for porn. Or solitaire, she thought wryly, as she moved the eight of spades to the next column.

"And he's really cool with just a one-night thing?" the brunette asked. "Like, I can even be up front about that?"

Riley almost snorted again. She didn't even need to know who he was to know that he was really cool with just a one-night thing.

"For sure," Sephora said. "This is what he's best at."

"One-night stands?"

"For just being all about the short-term fun. It's like…eating dessert for dinner. Not something you'd want to do all the time, but once in a while it's fun and makes you realize that you shouldn't take everything so seriously all the time." Sephora sighed. "No one should have to eat salad for *every* meal."

"Zach was salad?" her friend asked.

Sephora nodded. "Zach was what I thought I *should* do. We'd been dating since our junior year. I mean, I just assumed we were *supposed* to get married. He was comfortable and good for me and…the same. No matter what I tried to add to it, it was still just salad."

Riley thought maybe she should feel at least mildly amused at the analogy. But the truth was, she totally understood Sephora. It was really easy to get caught up in a salad life. It wasn't *bad*. In fact, it seemed like a good idea. It was certainly nothing anyone would judge. But at the same time, you could add croutons and Craisins all over the place, it was still just a bunch of lettuce underneath.

But dessert…that was a whole other thing. There were so many different kinds, different flavors, different experiences to be had with a dessert menu.

"But if you eat it for every meal, even chocolate could get old, right?" Curly asked. "So it's good that this guy is a short-term thing."

"Maybe," Sephora said. "But I sure wouldn't mind *trying* to get sick of his *chocolate*, if you know what I mean."

Curly and Riley both knew what she meant.

Who was this guy? Riley couldn't wait to see. And to see if she knew him. Because if she did, she *had* to find out if he knew about this reputation. Either the guy was brilliant and had cultivated this reputation and was, she had to admit, using it for a greater good in helping women get their mojo back. Or he was...brilliant and had marketed a bunch of B.S. that was getting him laid on a regular basis and praised in small town bars across the county.

There simply weren't enough jilted, or even single, women in Sapphire Falls to keep him *this* busy.

These women weren't from here. They were within two years on either side of Riley's twenty-six, and if they were Sapphire Falls girls she would have known them. Hell, she would have known them no matter how old they were. Or *of them* at least. Sapphire Falls was tiny and no one got away with being reclusive. Plus, Sephora was not a reclusive kind of girl. That was clear.

Riley focused on her computer screen again, but couldn't care less about the card game in front of her. *Keep going, Sephora. Tell us more.*

"He sounds amazing," Curly said, almost wistfully. "How do you leave the next morning? Don't you want more?"

Ooh, good question. Did the guy have stalkers all over the tri-county area now? Were women yearning and longing and weeping over no longer having him and his Cock of Wonder?

"Oh, no. It's pretty easy to leave in the morning," Sephora said.

"Oh?"

Sephora nodded. "He'll give you every fantasy that night, but the next day he says goodbye, hands you a cup of coffee and walks you out to your car." She paused and then added, "He seriously has like fifteen flavors of coffee to choose from and like eight flavors of creamer and syrups. You can have whatever kind you want. But he also has a stash of disposable coffee cups with lids in his kitchen. So, you get the coffee fixed exactly the way you want it, and then you take it with you."

Riley had to cover her laugh with a cough. Oh my God, who *was* this guy? Because she was kind of impressed. Maybe a little horrified, but mostly impressed. Because it sounded like the women knew exactly what they were getting into, agreed to it, and had a hell of a good time. And then got coffee.

"So, don't even think about dating him," Curly said. "Got it."

"Yeah, don't get attached," Sephora agreed. "Though, really, I don't think that's a risk."

"No?" Curly said. "He sounds amazing."

Riley wasn't so sure that *amazing* was the word she'd use, but he was intriguing.

"He's hot-fling material," Sephora said. "Not boyfriend material. Once you get past the orgasms, and look around his apartment and stuff, you'll realize he's a confirmed bachelor and would be way too much work to convert."

Okay, well, trying to *convert* anyone into anything else was always a bad idea, but Riley was glad this woman was cautioning her friend against even trying.

"Is it a dump?" Curly asked.

"Not really. It's just very...male. He has a few kinds of body wash you can pick from in his bathroom, and he has nice towels and stuff. I thought that was interesting," she said. "But the rest of the place...looks like a guy lives there with no female influence at all."

The guy gave these women a choice of coffee creamer *and* body wash at his place? Good Lord. Riley had to admit that impressed was starting to edge out horrified. He was kind of a master. And the disposable, to-go coffee cups? Brilliant.

The door to the Come Again opened just then and Riley realized Sephora was facing the door. No doubt waiting to spot the Sex God. Though Riley thought the guy really should walk around with a T-shirt proclaiming him as such. Or something. Did the guy glow? Did he have a halo over his head for all the good he was doing for the area women?

"Oh!" Sephora gasped. "There he is."

Riley almost hurt her neck snapping it around to see who had come through the door.

But the next second, she frowned.

No. That couldn't be right. The woman must be confused. Because the guy who had just walked into the Come Again was Derek Wright. The bartender. Riley's brother's best friend. The guy she thought of as a second brother. Her second, even more annoying brother, to be exact. The guy who had once put dead spiders in her bed. She'd kicked his ass for that. Of course, then he'd been scrawny and a lot shorter than he was now.

"Oh my God, he's gorgeous," Curly said.

Riley looked from her and then in the direction she was staring. But no, she was still looking at Derek.

"I know, right?" Sephora said. "Look at those shoulders."

So, Riley did. But they were just shoulders. On Derek. The guy who, when she was eight and he was twelve, put all of her Barbies in compromising positions with Kyle's army guys all over her bedroom. She remembered being shocked that Derek had known those positions. In fact, looking back now, she was still a little shocked.

She narrowed her eyes and studied the guy that she'd known her entire life. Literally. He'd been there when her parents had brought her home from the hospital as a newborn. He'd lived next door and decided that where there was excitement and cake, he too would be.

But Sex God? She winced. She wasn't sure she should know the stuff she now knew about him. Or that she wanted to.

Then again, maybe the girls were looking at someone else at the bar. It was Tuesday night, so it wasn't like it was packed, but there were three other guys up there. Of course, one was her brother, Kyle. And she did *not* want to know if the girls were talking about him.

But it couldn't be Kyle. For one, he didn't live in a house, he lived over at Ty Bennett's place, a sort-of boarding house type setup. He was building a house, but it was far from finished. For another, he worked horribly long and erratic hours as the town physician, so he'd hardly have time for all of this Good Samaritan screwing. Even before Hannah, his one true love, had walked back into his life. Which she had. So no, it wasn't Kyle.

But maybe they were talking about—

"So that, my friend, is Derek Wright. The man who is going to change your whole sad, post-break-up perspective," Sephora said.

Well, crap. So much for pretending they were talking about someone else.

"Okay," Curly said with a nod. "But, why is he all muddy?"

Riley looked back over to where Derek was now leaning on the bar. He was the main bartender here, but the business belonged to Bryan Murray, who was currently behind the bar. Derek was leaning on his forearms, laughing with the guys, including Bryan and Kyle. And Curly was right. He was muddy. Not as in his shoes were muddy from being outside. He was muddy from the ass down. And it looked like he had streaks of mud on his arms and even his face. What the hell was that about?

And for reasons she couldn't quite explain, Riley pushed up out of her chair and headed in that direction. As she approached Derek, her mind swirled with all of the things she'd overheard. He was well-known for his short-term flings? He made women feel better after their breakups? He was. .a Sex God? He had flavored coffee creamers in his kitchen?

No freaking way.

"Can I talk to you?" she asked, walking right up to him and interrupting whatever conversation was going on between the guys.

Derek looked over at her and lifted a brow. "Me?"

She rolled her eyes. She was looking right at him. "Yes, you."

"Uh, yeah. Okay."

Uh, yeah. Okay. Well, she could believe the part about him not being much of a talker. He did, indeed, fit the stereotype of the guy who was pretty much about sports, hunting, and fishing. Which were also technically sports, so...sports. He was all about sports. Not technological advances, not math and science, not world-wide communications and cooperation. He was into throwing balls and killing things.

And orgasms. She couldn't forget the orgasms.

Even though she seriously wanted to.

"Riley?" Derek waved a hand in front of her face.

She blinked and shook her head. Dammit. Why did *he* have to be the Sex God?

"In back?" she asked.

Now he looked more interested and maybe even a touch concerned. "Okay."

He straightened from the bar, and she was hit by how not-scrawny he was now. No way could she kick his ass for anything. He was six-two or three, lean, muscled—yeah, yeah, his arms were impressive—and...damn, his shoulders really were wide.

"You alright?" Kyle asked.

He was slightly behind her, because Riley had been solely focused on Derek and had shoved in right between them. She looked over her shoulder. "Yeah. Of course. Just need to ask Derek something."

Are you aware of the Sex God title? How the hell did that happen? What's wrong with you? Do you really want to only be known for that? And are you using condoms? Because that's a really good way to get a disease that could make your miraculous cock dry right up and fall off.

And she'd just thought of Derek's cock as miraculous.

No. She could not handle this. This was not okay.

Derek headed for the back room through the swinging door behind the bar. Riley took two seconds to breathe deeply and rein in her stupid, disturbing thoughts—like the one where a plastic soldier was on his knees with his face between Barbie's legs—and started after him.

Okay, they were not going to talk about sex. No way. All of this was none of her business. Derek could do whatever he wanted with whoever he wanted. If his dick caught the plague and fell off, that was his own fault.

But he had multiple kinds of coffee and body wash for his "overnight guests"? That was kind of...nice. Or something. Sure, he was booting them out as soon as the sun rose, but he was being considerate about it. Or as considerate as a guy handing a woman a disposable coffee cup that said it's-not-you-it's-me-don't-call-me-and-I-won't-call-you could be.

And hey, Sephora hadn't seemed upset. He'd helped her move on. He'd practically done charity work, to hear her tell it.

"What's up?" he asked with a frown the second Riley came through the swinging door into the kitchen area.

"Isn't that a health code violation or something?" she asked, gesturing to his muddy jeans and boots.

"You're worried about the cleanliness of my kitchen?" he asked.

Of course she wasn't worried about his kitchen. She wasn't really worried about anything. Except maybe...him. Or his reputation. Or his STD status. All of which was completely ridiculous.

"Well, I *eat food* out of this kitchen. I'd like to know it doesn't have earthworms in it."

Derek gave her a little half smile. "You've eaten worse."

She sighed. Well, she wasn't sure it was *worse* than earthworms. He'd put smashed-up ants in her peanut butter once. Then she narrowed her eyes. She knew about the ants. It was very possible that he'd done something worse that she *didn't* know about.

"I don't want to know," she said.

"You're right," he told her with a nod.

Well, he might have a magic cock, but he was still kind of a dick.

––––––

"Why are you all muddy?" Riley asked, looking him up and down with her very familiar you're-such-a-dumbass look.

Derek had gotten that look from her probably a million times in his life. It still made him grin. "Because I fell in the mud."

She sighed.

To be honest, he played up the dumbass stuff for Riley's benefit. She'd always been a too-smart, geeky know-it-all, and he'd loved playing the big dumb buffoon who wasn't worthy to even engage in conversation with her. She loved to spout off about politics and climate change and women's rights and the arts. And if she got started on technology and social media, she could talk the Pope to drink.

It wasn't that Derek didn't care about those things or have opinions, but the girl had always used big words on purpose—with a snotty, you're-not-worthy tone of voice—and loved to debate and, frankly, she was exhausting.

So whenever he'd been around her, from about age twelve to, well, now, he just played along that he didn't have a clue. That way, Riley got to feel smart, and he didn't have to get into a conversation that would take many, many, *many* precious minutes off of his life.

Thing was, he agreed with her. On just about every point she made. So what was the point in talking about it?

"I was out at the cemetery. Don didn't get the new section mowed earlier so he called to see if I could do it."

"You fell off the lawnmower?" she asked, her tone indicating she had no trouble believing that he was incapable of even mowing grass.

Jesus, she was a pain in his ass. "I was helping Lucy, actually." He smiled thinking of the other too-smart geek he'd known most of his life. Unlike Riley, her best friend Lucy was sweet and quiet, and the only time she'd ever made him feel dumb was during her Valedictorian speech, when she'd quoted people he'd never heard of and said things that went right over his head. Fortunately, 99.5% of the audience in the Sapphire Falls high school gymnasium bleachers had been in the same boat, so he hadn't felt so bad.

But he'd realized in that moment that Lucy and Riley were out of his league. Sure, Riley got not-great grades, but he knew she was smart. Very smart. And cool and funny and beautiful. And he'd been giving her a hard time pretty much her entire life. They might have been geeks who didn't date much and spent most of their weekends in Riley's basement, but yeah, they were on a whole other level from Derek and the girls he hung out with.

Not that his big-brother-ish teasing had stopped that day. He and Riley had their relationship very well established by then. And, well, clearly she didn't need him giving her pep talks or telling her she was awesome or encouraging her to go after her dreams. So, he told himself she needed him to keep her grounded.

"You were helping Lucy?" Riley repeated. "At the cemetery?"

"Yep. I'd just gotten done mowing and she was there looking at headstones for some town history thing she's doing."

Lucy ran the local bookstore and was in charge of the town's archives. She also oversaw the Sapphire Falls town museum—an old house on Main that served, more or less, as a storage unit for people's old clothes, books, photos and other "items". Most of the stuff in there was just old, but everything supposedly had a story that tied it to the founding families. Derek wasn't so sure about the validity of those claims, but the museum was Lucy's headache, not his.

Except, of course, when something leaked—like a pipe or the roof—or a big heavy bookcase needed to be moved from the third story to the first. Or when a big heavy table needed to be moved from the first floor to the third. Or when big heavy boxes needed to be retrieved from, or stored in, the attic. Or when everything needed to be moved around for the haunted house.

The old house was the site of the traditional haunted house at Halloween and during the annual town festival every June. No one knew why they had a haunted house during the summer festival, but it was tradition, so they did. Which meant that twice a year, Derek was the main guy helping put it all together. And take it all down.

Of course, Lucy thought the place was *actually* haunted and had data on whose ghosts inhabited the oldest house in town.

Derek shook his head. Lucy was sweet and...quirky. That was really the best word for her. And she was cute. That he couldn't deny. She'd grown from nerdy-bookworm cute into shy-librarian cute. He wasn't sure what the exact distinction between the two was, but he was pretty sure it had something to do with her losing the baggy hoodies that hid her curves, her use of lip gloss that called attention to her very nice lips, and her increased confidence that resulted in more eye contact and smiles.

"And you ended up in the mud how?" Riley asked.

Derek focused on the pain-in-the-ass redhead in front of him instead of thinking about sweet Lucy's lip gloss. "I slipped down an embankment over in the oldest part of the cemetery."

He looked down. A little mud never hurt anyone. "But I'm good with being dirty."

He was shocked to see Riley blush.

For one, he wasn't sure he'd ever seen Riley blush. For another...what had he said?

"So, anyway, did you need something?" he asked.

He stripped off his shirt and turned toward the back door. He had a duffle hanging on a hook back there that had extra clothes in it. He had extra clothes stored in a lot of places— here, his truck, his grandmother's house, and over at Kyle's, since Kyle lived in town, at least right now.

It seemed Derek was always in need of a clean shirt or jeans. He did odd jobs all over town and very few of them were actually scheduled. Or paid, for that matter. He never knew when he might get called to help someone change a tire, or pull out a tree stump, or dig their fishing boat out of the mud. He didn't mind that everyone in town had his cell number and used it freely. He was easily bored, didn't like to sit still, and loved not having a set schedule.

Of course, once the pizza ovens were finished at the Come Again and they got that business up and going, he'd be busier with work there, but hey, it was pizza. It wasn't like he was spending his days saving lives at the hospital like his best friend Kyle, or protecting the town like his buddy Scott, one of Sapphire Falls' cops. Derek's specialties were pizza and beer, and that was just fine with him. He was an expert in both.

Riley still hadn't said anything, so he turned back after he'd pulled a clean shirt from his bag.

She was staring at him as if she'd never seen him before. He frowned and yanked the T-shirt over his head. "What's wrong with you?" he asked, pulling the shirt into place and tucking the dirty one into his bag.

She shook her head. "Nothing. I'm fine. I'm..." She seemed to be searching for words. Then she frowned, planted her hands on her hips and said, "There's a woman out front looking for you. I thought I'd warn you."

Riley was warning him about a woman? That was...weird. For one, Riley had never been protective of him in all the time he'd known her. For another... Nope, pretty much just that one thing. She loved when he screwed up and fell on his ass—figuratively and literally.

And "as long as he'd known her" was a really long time. He'd been there when her parents had brought her home from the hospital. He'd only been four but he remembered it distinctly. She had been crying her lungs out when they'd carried her into the house, and he'd thought "holy shit, she's gonna be a pain". Okay, maybe he hadn't thought the word "shit" at that tender age, but he did remember thinking that Riley had seemed like more trouble than she was worth from the very first minute.

But he'd stuck around anyway. Because her grandmother had made a strawberry cake. And Ruby's cakes had always been worth putting up with Riley. Thankfully. Because Riley had always been there. Kyle's birthday parties, neighborhood gatherings, Super Bowl parties, *Derek's* birthday parties. He hadn't been able to get rid of her.

Thank God for Ruby's cakes.

Riley's It's-A-Girl cake had been pink with pink frosting and one of the best things he'd ever tasted in his life. He assumed that was why he'd always associated strawberries with Riley, and why he'd called her Shortcake when they'd been growing up. It was definitely why it had amused him so much when she'd dyed her hair red when she'd turned fourteen. She'd gone from a mousy brown to a fiery look-at-me red. And the guys had definitely looked.

He was pretty sure they hadn't stopped looking since.

It wasn't just the red hair. She had several piercings in her ears, one in her nose, and one in her belly button. She had tattoos—gorgeous ones that ran up the entire length of one leg and showed off her creamy skin when she wore shorts or skirts one on her shoulder that peeked out with certain tops, and one on her lower stomach that he hadn't seen but he'd heard Peyton telling Scott about.

Riley was also gorgeous, had a trim body with big boobs. and an attitude that said "I dare you". And all of that would have made him follow her around like a puppy if it weren't for two very important facts.

One, he'd known her his whole life, and she was like an annoying little sister to him.

Two, she didn't really like him.

She seemed like a rebel. She'd gone with the piercings and tattoos—using fake ones until she was old enough to get real ones—in order to get away from her big brother's Boy Scout reputation. Kyle had huge shoes to fill, and Riley had grown tired of being "Kyle Ames's little sister" very early on. So she'd started acting out and expressing herself...differently than Kyle had. Kyle's straight A's, perfectionistic, straight-laced habits were countered with Riley's barely passing grades—in spite of her high IQ and giftedness in math and computer science—lots of swearing, and general antisocial tendencies. Kyle had been involved in everything. Riley had hung out in her parents' base-ment with three computers and an online community no one else really knew about or understood.

So yeah, Riley *seemed* to be Derek's type, but women who didn't like him were definitely *not* his type.

"What's she look like?" he asked of the woman supposedly looking for him.

"Well, there are two actually. A brunette and a blond." Riley tipped her head and narrowed her eyes. "She's basically looking for you so you can help her friend get over a breakup."

Huh. Brunette and blond didn't really narrow it down. "What did she say?"

"That you—" Riley faltered, blushed, coughed, then said, "Apparently you two spent the night together and she never thought about her ex again."

Also didn't really narrow it down, but Derek was far too distracted by Riley's reaction to the whole thing. She was fucking *blushing*. Again. What the hell? And she'd dyed her hair red from brown, but she did have the pale skin of a redhead. Which made the pink staining her cheeks all the more obvious.

"Oh," he said, searching for something to say other than "that sounds about right."

"You don't seem surprised."

"About what?"

"That her heartbreak was totally healed after one night with you, and she was able to move on, happier, more confident, and feeling good about herself."

He shrugged. "That's kind of how it should work, right?"

"How what should work?"

"Really hot sex with someone who thinks you're amazing."

Her cheeks turned a darker pink, but that didn't completely distract from her very skeptical look. "They *all* think you're amazing? After knowing you only one night?"

Derek realized this was the most bizarre conversation he and Riley had ever had. "Well, as you can attest, I probably seem more amazing the *less* time you know me."

But instead of agreeing with him, she frowned.

Then before she could respond, he said, "And actually, I was referring to how *I* make *them* feel."

Her frown deepened. "What do you mean?"

He shrugged. "I want *them* to feel amazing."

"Because then they'll go and talk about you to all of their girlfriends?"

Derek shook his head. Why did she care? "Look, I'm like... Vegas," he said.

Riley's eyebrows went up. "You're like Vegas?" she repeated. "What does that mean?"

"People love Vegas," Derek said. "Vegas has the reputation of being an anything-goes, get-away-from-it all, if-it-feels-good-do-it hell of a good time, right?"

"Okay," Riley said slowly.

"But no one wants to *live* there, you know? And even the people who go regularly don't stay for long and go back to their real lives in between."

He watched Riley process all of that.

"You understand?" he finally asked her.

She nodded, looking slightly stunned.

"And if you come home from Vegas and *didn't* have a great time, and don't feel a little better about facing your real life, and don't smile thinking back on your time there, then you did something wrong," he said.

Again, she nodded, with a slight frown. "So...you're like Vegas," she repeated again.

Satisfied that she understood, Derek nodded. "I'm like Vegas."

Her frown deepened. "Why do you want to be like Vegas?" she asked. "That's about as opposite from Sapphire Falls as you can get, and you love it here."

He did. Definitely. But... "Pretty much every other guy here is Sapphire Falls," he said.

She looked confused.

Derek sighed. "Everyone here is about family and settling down and putting down roots and being a part of this big community. Which I love," he added. "But the women here can basically throw a rock and hit a nice guy who wants to put up a white picket fence and start having babies. And most of the women want that. And that's great. But some-times they just need something else. Like a quick trip to Vegas."

Riley's eyes widened and she said, "Dessert instead of salad."

He frowned but decided he didn't need to understand that. "So, anyway, I'll go out and talk to these ladies and see if they're up for some gambling this weekend." He gave Riley a cocky wink that he knew would annoy her.

She frowned on cue. "It's just the one girl who needs to get over a breakup."

"Well, it's not uncommon to show up in Vegas, thinking you know which game is yours and have your mind totally changed by the lights and glitter." He had no intention of taking two women home, but again, he loved the idea of shocking Riley a little.

Her eyes narrowed. "I don't suppose any of this has anything to do with the fact that women who have just been through a breakup are easy targets, right? Their self-esteem is low so you come along, act a little romantic, and they'll fall for anything?"

Derek felt his own frown forming. He and Riley had always poked at each other, teased, pointed out each other's flaws readily. But *this* felt more...something. More raw. More annoying. More real.

"You know, you can be a real brat sometimes." He pulled his hand from his pocket and started toward the door.

"Where are you going?"

"Out of this kitchen," he told her shortly.

"Hey—"

He swung back even as he knew he should just keep going. "What?"

"Do you remember Sarah Lamb?" she asked.

Derek frowned at the out-of-the-blue question. "Of course."

"You mean, of course you remember taking her virginity. In *my* basement."

Well...yeah. And he knew that Riley thought of the basement in her parents' house as hers. It was where she'd spent nearly all of her out-of-school time. But once in a while, Kyle and his friends would commandeer the away-from-the-parents space.

And if she thought Sarah was the only girl he'd had sex with down there, she'd be very wrong.

"I do remember that," he said hesitantly. Because he sensed there was more.

"Do you remember laughing and talking about her and my other friends two years before that?"

He shook his head. "No."

"Sarah and Lucy and Kate were spending the night. Sarah had a huge crush on you, and Kyle told you that. Then you laughed and said, 'What would I talk to a girl like that about if we were alone for even five minutes?' We were upstairs in the kitchen getting drinks, and we heard you."

Derek blew out a breath. "Shit. I'm sorry. I didn't know that."

"She was so embarrassed. She didn't come over for months after that because she was afraid of seeing you, and you were *always* at our house." Riley was frowning at him as if this had happened just last night.

"I'm sorry." He shrugged. "I really am. I didn't know she heard me. I didn't even know she was up there." He paused. He knew he shouldn't go on but, he couldn't help himself. "But seriously, Riley, what *would* we have talked about?"

Riley drew herself straighter. "You weren't worried about that two years later in my basement."

And, also knowing he should *not* say it, he replied easily, "Well, we weren't *talking* much that night."

Then he turned and headed back out front, done with this conversation. And done with letting Riley get to him. For now.

Because she *always* got to him.

2

____

"So basically, you want to have sex with me," Scott said to Derek as Derek set a beer down in front of him.

"That is absolutely *not* what I said," Derek told him. He looked at Kyle. "You get what I'm saying, right?"

Kyle nodded. "Sure. But if you want to have sex with one of us, I don't know why it isn't me."

These two were his best friends, and he'd known he was going to get shit about this. But if they hadn't given him a rough time, he would have thought they weren't really taking him seriously. "I don't want to have sex with either of you," Derek said firmly but calmly.

"But you said that you have no women in your life like us." Scott waggled his thumb back and forth between himself and Kyle. "But you'd like to have the kind of sex you're having now with someone *like* that."

Derek gave him a look that said, "I know you're being a dumbass on purpose." He sighed. "I want to have hot sex with a woman who knows me the way you two know me." He held up a hand before either of them said anything. "I want to have someone like Peyton or Hannah."

There. *That* would make it clear what he was talking about. Peyton and Scott knew each other inside and out and were still having rock-the-house sex all the time. Hannah and Kyle had known each other and been in love since high school. They had a history that was both awesome and a little painful, and they were as close as any couple Derek had ever seen. And they were as hot together as Peyton and Scott.

Derek knew—in fact, he was pretty sure he'd been the one to point out to these guys—that when you were with someone who knew you well, and loved you in spite of knowing you well, the sex was even better. He knew that. He'd had something very close to that a couple of times. He didn't take on the whole I-want-to-be-your-everything bit that Scott and Kyle did, so even the relationships with the couple of women he'd been serious about weren't as all-consuming as what Scott and Peyton and Kyle and Hannah were doing. There was no way Derek wanted to be anyone's everything. That was a hell of a lot of pressure. But he did know that sex with a woman he truly cared about and knew well was amazing and...well, other things were amazing too. Like spending time outside of the bedroom. Something he didn't do with women very often.

But maybe he should. Maybe it was time to have a longer-term relationship. Maybe it was time to get serious. It was sure working well for Scott and Kyle.

Of course, Scott and Kyle were the more serious types by nature. Definitely. Kyle was a straight-laced, perfectionistic physician, and Scott was a by-the-book, save-the-world cop. Derek was...a playboy bartender.

It probably wasn't great for him to model his whole life after these guys. He didn't think he could be a rule-following perfectionist if someone paid him a million bucks to do it.

So why was he all of a sudden thinking about his relationships with women?

But the answer was obvious. And annoying.

Riley.

The talk with Riley three nights ago had replayed in his mind for hours afterward. And he was pissed the next morning when he'd awoken tired. And alone. He hadn't gone out to talk to the women who'd been there looking for him. He'd told his friends he needed to get cleaned up from the mud and had headed home. Where he'd proceeded to think about the fact that Riley obviously thought he was an ass about women, and had been since high school when he'd debauched her basement couch.

He frowned. And now he was thinking about her *again*. Why did he care what Riley thought of him? He wasn't a dumb kid—or a dumb early-twenty-something guy—anymore. He'd grown up. He was doing shit with his life. He was an integral part of the community, was close to his family, had a job he loved, and lots of friends. He was happy. His situation was damned near perfect. It didn't matter if Riley knew any of that or believed it. She wasn't actually his little sister. He wasn't even sure he'd call her a friend.

Yet, he was still pissed that she thought he hit on women with broken hearts because they were easier. He wasn't an asshole. And he didn't need easy, thank you very much.

Scott took a swallow of beer. "Well, sorry, buddy, can't help you there. Peyton is very taken."

"Yeah, I'm pretty sure I've ruined Hannah for any other man," Kyle said.

Clearly neither of them actually thought Derek was talking about having sex with *their* girls, but he sighed anyway. "Thanks for the talk, guys."

His friends were absolutely head over heels in love. The whole let's-get-a-dog-and-spend-every-Christmas-together-and-tell-each-other-everything kind of love, but they were also having Vegas-worthy sex. It could be done.

Not that this was all some great revelation to Derek. It

might shock Riley Ames, but he was actually a pretty insightful guy.

"Look," Kyle finally said, setting his coffee cup aside and leaning in—the sure sign he was *finally* going to give Derek some real input. "You think you're Vegas to all these girls who are stuck in Sapphire Falls. You think you're giving them this short-term good time when things in their real life get a little boring or don't work out the way they plan. But I think what you have to ask yourself is...how much do *you* need the regular trips to Vegas."

Derek refilled Kyle's cup, thinking that over. It wasn't quite time to switch the bar over from alcohol to coffee and tea only something he did every night around midnight, but Kyle was on call pretty much twenty-four seven. It wasn't unusual for him to not drink, no matter what time it was.

"You think I'm doing all of that for me more than for them?" Derek asked.

"You send them back out into Sapphire Falls," Kyle said. "You help them let loose for a night, or a weekend, or even for a few weekends, but eventually they go back to their real lives. find nice guys, and settle down. And everyone knows that's what's going to happen."

"Because that's what they ultimately want," Derek said. "Nobody wants Vegas all the time."

"Except you."

Derek felt himself freeze. He looked at Kyle. "What?"

"You're the one who doesn't go back out into the 'regular' dating scene after one of your flings." Kyle picked up his cup and sipped with that smug look he often got when he was right about something.

Derek didn't really know what to say to Kyle's revelation.

"But he does go back out into regular life in Sapphire Falls," Scott said. "I mean, it's not a relationship, but Derek is as Sapphire Falls as it gets. All the odd jobs around town, running the main social hub, involved in everything, knows everyone." Scott regarded Derek with a thoughtful look. "Yeah, maybe those 'Vegas trips' are for you as much as they are for the women. It's a way to let loose and get out of the regular grind around here and then, Monday morning, you're back to being committed to your longest-term, most serious relationship." He nodded as if figuring it all out. "You can't be serious about a woman because you're already in a committed relationship. With this town."

Derek felt his eyes narrow. But he didn't hear himself arguing.

Was he avoiding commitment in a relationship because he was already over-committed to...everything else in his life?

"I think I just really like the hot sex with beautiful, willing partners who think I'm amazing," he finally said.

Scott shrugged. "Or maybe it's just that."

"Yeah, that makes sense too," Kyle said, picking up his cup again.

Derek rolled his eyes. Yeah, these guys were a ton of help.

"Officer, I'm here to report a crime."

Peyton Wells, Scott's girlfriend, slid between Scott and Kyle, her body rubbing against Scott's. The big cop grinned down at her. "Yeah, what happened?"

"You're going to have to cuff me and frisk me before I talk," she told him.

"That can be arranged." Scott pivoted on the stool and settled his hands possessively on her hips. "Though I don't know where you'd be hiding any weapons in this outfit."

Peyton was, as usual, dressed in short shorts and a tank that fit her body like a glove. She was Scott's, completely and without a doubt, but as a red-blooded straight man, Derek had to admit that Peyton was damned nice to look at.

"Oh, I think I might have a thing or two that I can use

against you," she told Scott with a smile that said very clearly to everyone looking on what she meant.

Scott gave a low growl and said, "I'm not going to get any work done on that paperwork tonight, am I?"

"Oh!" Peyton leaned back slightly. "I forgot about that! You are *definitely* going to get work done on that."

Scott pulled her close again. "I don't want to work on it."

"I'll reward you afterward." Peyton batted her eyes at him and licked her bottom lip.

Scott started to lean in to kiss her, but she pulled back at the last second.

"*After*."

"Dammit, Trouble," Scott grumbled.

"You have to get that in by next Friday," she said. "Seriously." She looked over at Derek and Kyle. "Tell him that he has to go do this presentation. He'll be so good at it."

"What presentation?" Derek asked.

"He didn't tell you?" She frowned up at Scott, then looked back to Derek. "He was asked to present at a multistate convention of law enforcement working on sex trafficking issues." She put a hand on Scott's cheek. "I know you *want* to do it. I'll help you with the paperwork. We'll get it done super-fast, and then you can..." She trailed off. "Whatever you want."

Derek actually felt the heat spiking between them. And he decided that, yes, *that* would be a very interesting thing to try— being with someone who knew his talents and dreams and encouraged them, even while tempting him with hot, handcuff-me-to-the-bed sex.

Then again, what talents and dreams did he have? Pizza ovens in the Come Again kitchen and maybe adding a couple of local microbrewery beers to the drink menu. And both of those things were going to be done in the next couple of months.

Huh. Maybe he didn't need a serious girlfriend because he didn't need any help being a better man.

And Riley floated through his mind again.

She would probably disagree.

No, she would *definitely* disagree.

He stubbornly resisted looking over at the table where she sat, her feet propped on the chair across from her, her laptop open, her headphones on—the universal signal for "I don't want to talk". She came in every night to work, just like a number of other people, including local bestselling author Michael Kade.

The Come Again had become an after-hours place for night owls who didn't have their own offices to work in. It had started because the work to expand the Come Again for the pizza business happened after the bar closed, and the lights had drawn Peyton in when she'd decided to take classes online. Other people had quickly noticed the lights and cars in the lot, and Derek had simply gone with it, keeping the coffeepot going until the wee hours.

Now it was just a routine, and he kind of liked it. His buddy Bryan Murray actually owned the bar, but Derek was going to be the owner of the pizza business, and he loved being a part of the Come Again. It really was the social hub of Sapphire Falls, and it mattered to him that he was a part of a place where people always felt welcome, where celebrations were held and defeats were made a little less painful, where you could come with a group of friends to make memories, or where you could come alone to make friends.

"Hey."

He focused again on the people in front of him as Hannah slid up onto the stool next to Kyle.

Kyle gave her a sweet kiss on the temple. "How was your day?"

She nodded, leaning in to rest against him. "Okay."

Kyle's hand rested on the back of her neck and he rubbed gently. Hannah had chronic neck pain from an accident a few years prior, and Derek wondered if Kyle even realized he was massaging her. It seemed an instinctive, protective action.

"You sound tired," Kyle said softly.

"I am."

"Okay, time to go home." He put his arm around her and started to stand. "Hot bath and then I'm tucking you in."

"And getting in with me?" she asked, giving him a sexy—if sleepy—smile.

"Just to sleep, Hannah," Kyle said. His expression was full of affection.

And Derek found himself having to swallow hard. On his right was the couple that had upped the temp in the whole bar just looking at each other, and on his left was the couple in which one was simply taking care of the other. And that was kind of hot...or something...too.

"This," he announced. Both couples looked at him. He gestured between them. "This is what I'm talking about."

Hannah, Kyle, Peyton and Scott all looked at one another, then back at Kyle. And Kyle and Scott nodded.

"Yeah, this is pretty great," Kyle said.

"You definitely want some of this," Scott added.

Yeah, he thought maybe he did. Vegas *and* Sapphire Falls all in one beautiful, sweet, naughty, fun package.

Kyle and Hannah said their goodnights and left. Peyton went up on tiptoe and whispered something in Scott's ear that had him saying goodnight a minute later.

And then Derek was alone.

He started wiping down glasses, lost in thought, until he heard, "Well, hey, I was hoping you were here tonight."

He looked up to find Ashley Archer leaning on the other side of the bar. "Hey, Ash. What's up?"

Ashley was a girl he'd "visited Vegas" with a couple of times. Maybe three. Or four.

"I was just wondering what you were up to this weekend?" She gave him a flirty smile.

He thought about it. He studied her lips. He thought about the last time they'd been together. Then he surprised them both and asked, "Have you read any of Michael Kade's books?"

Ashley frowned. "Um, no. Not really my thing."

Well, at least she knew who Kade was. He was living here in Sapphire Falls now though, and Derek wondered if she'd known the author before he moved in and started making a big deal about writing a tongue-in-cheek murder mystery set in Aquamarine Ridge, a town that bore an uncanny similarity to Sapphire Falls.

But Derek didn't ask. Because he didn't really want to know. He was about to ask a woman on a date, and he didn't really need to know that it was a dumb idea.

"He's hosting a thing here in town in a few weeks," Derek said. "It's a murder-mystery thing where fans can come to Sapphire Falls and actually live out the story in his book."

Derek thought it was fabulous. That would probably surprise a lot of people, but he was an avid reader and was, admittedly, a fan-boy dork over Michael Kade's stuff. He'd loved the Aquamarine Ridge book. It was funny and suspenseful with just enough gore. And he couldn't wait for the fan weekend. He was the guy building the sets they needed and the keeper of the weapons and clues, and he was stupidly into it.

That would surprise Riley, he bet.

And *dammit*, there he was thinking about her again.

"I heard something about the weekend thing," Ashley told him.

"Yeah, I'm working on the planning and everything. Was

wondering if you'd want to go to his book reading next Sunday afternoon?"

Kade was going to be reading from the book and signing copies at Lucy Geller's bookstore in town. The first hour was for Sapphire Falls only, then it would be open to anyone who wanted to make the trip to the little town. They were expecting a huge crowd, and every place from the diner to the bakery was gearing up to serve and charm their visitors. Hailey Conner Bennett, the woman in charge of everything having to do with tourism in Sapphire Falls, was nearly beside herself.

"A Sunday afternoon?" Ashley asked, as if he'd just asked if she knew how to tap dance.

It was true that most of his "dates" were long over by Sunday afternoon, and he was typically either at the pond fishing or lounging on his couch watching TV.

"Yeah, it starts at three," he said, telling himself he couldn't bail on the invitation just because she looked completely confused.

"Um..." Ashley glanced around. "I haven't read the book."

"You can still get a signed copy," Derek said, giving her a little smile. "You could get it read before the big murder-mystery event."

It wasn't much of a mystery, really. If people had read the book they knew how it would turn out. But they were still expecting a big crowd of people who wanted to live the book by seeing the places that Kade had described in the story and meet the people who had inspired some of the characters. Like local millionaire Levi Spencer, who had ended up as a sidekick to the detective in the story because of his near nightly negotiations—i.e., whining—with Kade. Of course, the sidekick had been brutally killed in chapter seven. But Levi thought that was the best thing ever and was now in negotiations with Hailey to let him use fake blood and stage the murder scene at City Hall himself.

And Derek couldn't forget the small-town doctor who doubled as the county's medical examiner and had been the one to blow the case wide open. None other than his buddy Kyle Ames. Who was *not* all that pleased with being the story's hero, because it meant that the doting fans would want to meet him. And dote on him.

It was all going to be a ton of fun. Derek couldn't wait.

But Ashley wasn't returning his grin. She shook her head. "I don't think so. But if you want to hang out Saturday night, let me know."

He knew what she meant by hang out, and he knew it did not involve a discussion about Kade's book. Or really a discussion of any kind, other than deciding who would start on the bottom. Got it. He nodded. "I'll let you know. Not sure what's up yet."

"Okay. See ya later."

Ashley walked away and Derek shook his head. Not only had he asked a woman on an actual date—and been turned down—but he realized that it was very likely the first time since he'd seen his first pair of breasts that *he'd* turned down sex.

Okay, he was technically just putting it off. It's not like he and Ashley needed to make concrete plans right now. He could still end up with her in his bed.

But he wasn't going to. He was going to ask someone else out.

And he blamed Riley Ames. Completely.

He shot a frown in her direction again, but she was completely oblivious to him.

Why did it matter what she thought?

Or rather, why did what she think of him influence what *he* thought of himself?

But suddenly he wanted to know that he could ask a woman out on a date and she'd want to go. A real date. Not hanging out as foreplay. Parties out at the river, dancing at a street dance, shooting pool here at the Come Again, even sitting at football games were all just a chance to flirt and do some major hinting. It was all foreplay. The lead up to sex. The opening act.

And now that Riley had gotten into his head, he really needed to prove that someone would want to go out with him even if that was all it was going to be.

He shoved a hand through his hair and looked around for something to do. But he had everything cleaned up. Dammit.

The door opened again and he looked up, hopeful. Maybe another of the girls he'd gone out with recently would come in and help reassure him that he was a nice guy who was good for something other than orgasms.

Lucy Geller stepped through the door—and Derek smiled. The universe didn't think he was *all* bad.

Lucy wasn't someone he'd gone out with before, but she was what he'd loosely call a friend. And she was nice.

Maybe that's what he needed. To *be* a nice guy, maybe he needed to hang out with nice girls. God knew, that would be something different. Not that the girls he spent time with were all bitches, but they weren't Lucy-nice. They were I'll-be-nice-and-suck-your-dick-on-the-drive-back-to-your-place nice.

He cleared his throat. Yeah, maybe to be a guy who did things other than have sex with the girls he took out, he needed to hang out with girls who didn't just want to have sex with him. And maybe that was best accomplished by spending time with someone he hadn't had sex with yet. Because—and he was only kind of bragging when he thought it—once they'd been in his bed, it might be hard to convince them they wanted to be anywhere else with him.

"Hey, Luce," he said.

She was wearing a pale-yellow sundress. Much like the one Riley was wearing. But where Riley had her arms and legs—and tattoos—exposed, Lucy was wearing a light sweater over hers. It was a far cry from the baggy sweatshirts, but it was still hard to really get a good look at her shape. Unlike Riley, where every curve was clearly on display.

Derek frowned at that. The *last* thing he needed on top of everything else was noticing how Riley filled out her clothes. Jesus.

"Hi, Derek."

Lucy gave him a sweet smile, and he purposefully focused on her lips. Yep, shiny peach lip gloss. And very nice lips underneath it.

"Can I get you something?" he asked.

Instead of a coy, flirtatious look like he so often got with that question, Lucy looked around the room. She spotted Riley and smiled. "Nope. I'm meeting Riley."

"No coffee? Nothing?"

Lucy looked back at him. "Oh. Um." She studied the chalkboard behind him where he had a few of the hot drinks he served at night listed. "Could you make cocoa?"

Cocoa. Yep, Lucy Geller was unlike the girls he usually hung out with. "Cocoa it is." He had chocolate syrup for the café mochas and chocolate martinis he served. "I'm guessing you're a whipped-cream kind of girl?" he asked with a wink.

She simply nodded. "That would be great."

Not a hint of a smile, not a teasing quip, nothing in response to the whipped-cream-kind-of-girl comment. Or the wink. She really just wanted whipped cream on top of her hot chocolate. Huh. Yeah, this was new.

She started in Riley's direction, and Derek noticed that Riley had her headphones off now and was watching them.

"Lucy," Derek said quickly before she got past the bar and within earshot of Riley.

She turned back. "Yeah?"

"I'm really looking forward to Kade's murder-mystery weekend."

Her brows rose, but she nodded. "Oh, me too."

Derek knew that Lucy was a huge Michael Kade fan. To the point that she stammered over her words and stumbled over her own feet in front of the author. It was adorable. "I was planning to be there on Sunday," he said of the book signing. "You need any help getting ready for it?"

She faced him fully. "Well, um...actually..."

She tucked her dark hair behind her ear, and Derek noticed that her fingers and her ear were both really small. That was a weird thing to notice, but it occurred to him that Lucy was very petite. She was probably only five-two or so, and he was 99% sure that she'd never worn a pair of high heels. It also occurred to him that this was the first time, other than the lip gloss thing the other day, that he'd ever really noticed her body.

"I'm happy to help with anything," Derek said quickly. Okay, it wasn't really asking her on a date, but it would be spending some time together, and he got the impression that working up to this with Lucy might be a good idea. If she didn't catch the teasing about whipped cream, then he was going to have to dial back his usual approach. Take it easy. Make a plan beyond "wanna do some shots and get naked?" Not that he ever said exactly that, but his reputation did a lot of talking for him.

"I could actually use a couple more hands," Lucy said.

See, if that had been Ashley saying that, he would have made some comment about hands and what she was doing with hers, along with some suggestions for his, but...this wasn't Ashley. Or Jeni. Or Anna. Or Abi. Or Madison. Or any of the other girls he would have also said that to.

"Just tell me what time to be there," he told her. Sincerity. That's what he'd try with her. Not that he was ever *not* sincere about doing shots and getting naked, but this was...different. And maybe different was good. Maybe it was exactly what he needed.

"How's noon?" Lucy asked.

He nodded. "Fine. But...let's have lunch beforehand. How's eleven?"

There. That was a *nice* invitation. There would be no shots, no nakedness. It would be a casual chance to get to know her a little...

Lucy blushed and tucked her hair behind her ear. Again. The same hair. That was already behind her ear. "Oh, I don't... you don't have to do that."

He watched her, a little confused. "I'd love to take you to lunch, Lucy," he said. Also sincerely.

She wasn't making eye contact now, and her cheeks were even brighter pink. What was it with women blushing around him lately? Women never blushed with him. At least, not the women he usually hung out with. Just Lucy. And Riley.

"I just—"

"Hey, honey." Suddenly Riley was right there beside Lucy. "You ready to get to work?"

"Um, yeah," Lucy said, almost seeming relieved. "I brought all the stuff."

"Great." Riley pointed to the table she'd just vacated. "Go on over. I'll get us something to drink."

"I ordered a hot cocoa," Lucy told her.

"Awesome. I'll bring it over." Lucy moved off and Riley whipped around to face Derek. "What are you doing?"

He frowned. "What? I'm not doing anything."

"Lucy looked completely uncomfortable." Riley narrowed her eyes. "What did you say to her?"

Derek felt the getting-familiar frustrated tension inching up his spine. "I asked if I could help with the book signing on Sunday."

Riley put a hand on her hip, looking highly suspicious. "How did you say it?"

"What are you talking about? I just asked if she needed any help."

"Did you say it like 'hey, Lucy, need any *help* on Sunday?'" Riley was, apparently, trying to imitate him. She'd dropped her voice and emphasized "help" in a this-might-mean-something-dirty way.

He sighed. "That doesn't sound like me."

She lifted a brow.

"No, I didn't say that. I didn't mean that either. I *sincerely*," there was that word again, "want to help if she needs it."

"She doesn't."

"She does," he said. "She said that she could use an extra pair of hands."

Riley sighed. "She didn't mean it like that."

"Like what?" But he knew what Riley meant. *She* got the way that could be flirtatious.

"What else did you say, Derek?" Riley actually seemed annoyed now.

"Okay, I was a huge asshole. Is that what you think?" he asked, annoyed too. "I offered my help—sincerely—and then asked her to lunch. What a dick, right?"

Riley stared at him. "You asked her to lunch?"

"Yes. Before we set up for the signing."

"Just the two of you?"

"Yes."

"So you asked her on a date."

He shrugged. "Yes."

Riley took two steps to the edge of the bar and pointed her index finger at him. "No."

He looked at her finger, then back to her face. "No? Seriously? Like I'm a dog?"

"You *are* a dog, Derek Wright," Riley said. "And you are forbidden to ask Lucy on a date."

"I'm *forbidden*?" He actually laughed at that. "By who?"

"Me."

"And what makes you think I'll listen to you?" he asked.

Her eyes narrowed, and she got a look on her face that actually made a chill go down his spine. "You don't want to mess with me, Derek," she said. "I've been to prison."

But he couldn't help it. He snorted. "You were in *jail*. And all the charges were cleared."

"Still."

"For a cybercrime. It's not like you killed anyone."

"Yet."

He leaned onto the bar across from her. "You're not so tough."

"I could make you *very* miserable."

Now *that* he kind of believed. "I want to take a nice girl to lunch. What's so wrong with that?"

"You're not good enough for her."

Okay. So *that* was exactly what he'd figured Riley thought of him. And it was maybe true. And it was what he kind of wanted to change. He blew out a breath and focused on Riley, letting *sincerity* show in his expression. He hoped.

"So, tell me how to be good enough."

Now it was her turn to snort. "Just give you a list and you'll do it?"

"Yeah." Why not?

"Why do you want to be good enough?" she asked, instead of answering.

"Maybe I think it's time for me to...be a better guy."

She seemed a little stunned by his answer. She frowned, then wet her lips. And for an instant, Derek noticed that *her* lips were pretty nice too.

He shook his head and focused. Wasn't that just like him to be thinking of another woman's lips mere minutes after asking another out? And *seconds* after saying he thought he should be a better guy.

"Lucy is a nice woman," he said. "And we live here in the

same town, have a ton of friends in common, have known each other for a long time. What's wrong with lunch?"

"She's not your type," Riley said.

"Exactly."

Riley studied his face for a long moment. "*You* want to turn over a new leaf? Or are you actually thinking that you'll show her what she's been missing?"

"You mean am I thinking about taking Lucy over to your mom and dad's basement?"

"Yeah," Riley admitted. "Is it bugging you that Lucy is one of the few women in town you haven't been with or something?"

He frowned. "Sarah was a *very* willing participant in all basement activities, Riley. I know you kind of love making me out to be this big bad guy, but every pair of panties that end up on my bedroom floor are put there by their owners."

She swallowed but then said, "That doesn't answer my question. Is Lucy appealing because her panties haven't been on your floor yet?"

"Maybe I'm thinking that I need to find out what all the hype is about, keeping panties *on*."

She chewed her bottom lip. Finally, she nodded. "I think you *do* need to learn that."

"So I have your permission?" he asked dryly.

Riley shook her head. "No."

"You can't stop me from asking her out."

"I can keep her from saying yes though," Riley said. "Trust me. Lucy listens to me, and she'll definitely listen if I tell her stay far away from you."

"You're a brat." And he meant *that* very sincerely.

"I know. But I care about my friends."

Finally, he scowled at her. "Did Sarah tell you something happened that night? Is that why it's such a big deal to you that I stay away from your friends?"

"It was more what happened *after* that night."

"What happened after that night?"

"You never called her or asked her out again."

Shit. He straightened and ran a hand through his hair. "No, I didn't. It was sex. That's it."

"Exactly."

"So she *wanted* me to take her out? Ask her on a date? Spend some time with her with her panties on?" he asked.

Riley was chewing her lip again. But she nodded.

"So why are you so against me doing those things with Lucy?"

"Because I don't actually think you know *how* to do those things," she told him. "I don't think you have any idea how to be a boyfriend. I don't think you know how to be with a nice girl."

Yeah, she was definitely a brat.

But she also had a point.

And he hated that.

"I've got hot chocolate to make," he said, pushing back from the bar. Hot chocolate. For a nice woman. Maybe the nicest he knew.

Riley seemed to hesitate, but finally she nodded. "I'll take one too," Riley told him as he turned away.

He was unable to keep from asking, "And are *you* a whipped-cream kind of girl?"

"I'm more of a melted-marshmallow girl." Then, seemingly out of the blue, she gave him a grin. "Even on my hot chocolate sometimes."

And damned if there wasn't a teasing glint in her eye. So *she* wasn't passing up the chance to tease about whipped cream. And more.

"You sure?" he asked. "I'm very good with a whipped cream can." Was he trying to see what she'd do or say to that? Yes. Yes, he was.

"Yeah, that's pretty much a given, Sex God," she said—and actually laughed.

Sex God. It might have been sarcastic, but Riley Ames had just called him a Sex God.

"Which is exactly why you should stay away from Lucy," she added, effectively taking him right back down a notch.

"Lucy's got enough whipped cream and Sex Gods in her life?" No one could really have enough of either, in Derek's opinion. Which might be the entire problem.

Riley just looked at him for a moment. "I think Lucy has exactly the right amount of both in her life."

Then she pivoted on her heel and headed for her table.

And Derek was left with a number of thoughts like *so the melted marshmallows aren't too hot then? And I could too be a good boyfriend. Probably. And Riley really does wear that dress well.*

Dammit.

3

———

"Everything okay?"

Riley realized she was scowling as she took her seat at the table with Lucy. She smiled and shook her head. "Sure. Derek just drives me nuts."

Lucy nodded, playing with her pencil. She looked worried.

Riley leaned in. "What's up?"

Lucy met her gaze. "I just..."

Oh, crap. Riley worked on not sighing. "Lucy? What's going on?" But she knew. Derek the Debaucher had gotten to her.

That had been stupidly easy for him.

"Derek asked me out," Lucy said.

Riley pretended she didn't already know that. "No kidding. When?"

"Just now when I was up at the bar."

Don't overreact. "What did you say?"

"I said he didn't have to do that."

Riley felt her scowl return. "He didn't have to do that? What's that mean?" He *shouldn't* have done it, but it wasn't like he was doing Lucy some big favor.

Lucy shrugged. "He offered to take me to lunch before he helps out with the book signing. I thought maybe he felt like he was supposed to make the offer."

"Why would you think that?"

Lucy pushed her glasses up her nose. "Well, I mean, he's never asked me to do anything social before. Why now?"

"Because you're lovely and he's finally pulling his head out of his ass and noticing?" Riley suggested.

Lucy laughed. "Well, that *would* be something."

Riley studied her friend. Yeah, it would. It would actually make her think more kindly toward Derek on one hand. If he was sincerely noticing that Lucy was great, that would say something good about him. But if he was just trying to have a perfect score with the women in Sapphire Falls...well, she'd have to kill him. And besides, it wouldn't be a *perfect* score. *She* was living here now, after all.

"Do you want to go out with him?" Riley asked.

"Oh, geez." Lucy sat back in her chair. "I wouldn't know what to do with a guy like that."

Derek was as different from Lucy as he could get, but Lucy was ten times smarter and a million times sweeter, and Derek should be the one worried about what *he* would do with *Lucy*. "What do you think you'd have to *do* exactly?" Riley asked. Was Lucy talking about sex? As in, she wouldn't know what to do during sex with a guy like Derek?

She wasn't really used to talking about guys with Lucy. They had so many things in common that there was never a shortage of topics, and they never really got around to guys. Because guys weren't that important to them.

Riley dated, but nothing serious. There had been two types of guys in Sapphire Falls—the ones who liked her but thought she was kind of a dork, and the ones who thought her rebellious side was hot and wanted to party with her. But she hadn't been a partier, and she hadn't been into guys who couldn't name at least four of the Avengers, so, she hadn't gone out much in high school. Once she'd ended up in California, things had changed a bit. Guys who could name *all* of the Avengers thought she was *interesting,* and she hadn't had to exert the rebellious thing as much away from her perfect big brother, so she'd found people like her and had enjoyed a fun dating life that sometimes involved sex and sometimes didn't. Like normal people did.

But Lucy had never left Sapphire Falls. She'd inherited her bookstore from her grandmother, along with a very nice trust fund that meant the bookstore didn't have to actually be profitable. She'd been a dork in high school too. But a happy dork. In fact, Lucy either didn't see that she was different, or she didn't care. And Riley loved that about her. Lucy did her thing, happily oblivious to the fact that other women their age were having relationships and getting married and having children.

"I'd have to go to ball games and stuff, right?" Lucy asked, looking at Riley through her big pink-rimmed glasses.

Riley couldn't remember a time when Lucy *hadn't* worn glasses. And they'd met in kindergarten. She shook her head and focused. Ball games. And stuff. With Derek. She nodded. "He *is* very into sports."

"And he might want to take me fishing or something," Lucy commented. She was fiddling with her pencil again.

Riley was sure that fishing with Derek didn't involve a lot of actual fish, but yeah, he might want to take Lucy "fishing". "He definitely likes to fish," Riley agreed.

"I don't know much about football or fishing," Lucy said. Then she scrunched her nose up. "I haven't watched football since junior high and I've never actually *been* fishing."

Good grief, Derek Wright was getting Lucy Geller to think about football and fishing. And she had no idea that they wouldn't be fishing at all. Riley was sure he could get her friend thinking about a lot of other things she hadn't really tried before as well. Yes, okay, Lucy was a grown woman. A very intelligent one. And as such, she had every right to decide who she spent time with and what they did during that time. But Lucy was also a sweet, somewhat naïve, geeky virgin. No, Riley and Lucy had never said the word "virgin" to one another, but Riley would put her next month's rent money—and she desperately needed that money, because she was saving up to get the hell out of her parents' house— down on Lucy being one. And that made Riley feel protective of her.

Riley noticed Derek coming toward their table with their cups of cocoa, and she refrained from replying to Lucy's comment. For now.

"Here you go, ladies." He set the cups down. "No whipped cream for Riley and *extra* for Lucy." He grinned at Lucy, then gave Riley a look that said giving Lucy extra and Riley none had everything to do with the innuendo in his tone—okay, both of their tones—when they'd been discussing whipped cream a little bit ago. Why she'd teased about not wanting whipped cream but liking melted marshmallows, she had no idea. It was as if Derek pulled flirting out of women even when they had no intention of bantering with him.

"This looks great." Lucy dipped her finger in the whipped cream and lifted it to her mouth as she looked up at Derek.

Riley was surprised at the playful move, then realized that Lucy hadn't meant it to be anything other than a taste of the whipped cream. She glanced up at Derek. He was staring at Lucy's mouth.

Oh, boy. She sighed. "Thanks, Derek. We'll let you know when we're ready for refills."

He looked over at her and arched a brow. He knew he was being dismissed. But he addressed Lucy when he said, "If you need more whipped cream, at any time, you know where to find me." Then he gave Riley a wink and headed back to the bar.

She frowned after him. He was just going to mess with Lucy right in front of her? Um, no.

"I don't think you should go out with him," she told Lucy.

Lucy set her mug down, licking whipped cream from her lip in a way that Riley was sure Derek would find completely hot. But Lucy didn't even realize she was doing anything flirtatious.

"You don't?" Lucy asked.

Riley couldn't let them hang out. Lucy would be giving off signals that weren't signals at all, and Derek would somehow manage to talk her into…fishing. Even if he claimed that he was interested in being a better guy, she wasn't convinced Derek could turn off the get-into-my-bed that seemed to ooze out of him.

He didn't really want a nice girl. Riley believed that he kind of, maybe, thought he did. He was watching Scott and Kyle settle down, and he was thinking that some of that might be nice. Hell, how could anyone be around Kyle and Hannah and *not* think that true love forever and ever amen was *the* ultimate goal in life? Throw Scott and Peyton on top of that and…yeah, she could see why Derek might be having some thoughts.

But she wasn't entirely convinced that he really, *really* wanted that. He might want to try it out, but that didn't mean it would be for him. It didn't mean that he wouldn't get into a relationship like that and realize it was a lot of responsibility, and it came with a lot of expectations that he wasn't quite ready to fulfill on a long-term, all-the-time basis. And she didn't want him practicing on Lucy.

She knew that he was dependable. The whole town depended on him for things. She knew that he was trustworthy. The whole town trusted him. He was very committed to Sapphire Falls and the people here. But there had to be a reason that none of that had ever transferred to a woman.

And yes, Riley should mind her own business. But she probably wasn't going to. Derek wasn't going to practice the relationship thing, and realize it wasn't for him, with Lucy. He could practice on someone else. Break someone else's heart. And if he ever got good at it and decided he *did* want to be serious, *then* he could ask Lucy out. Maybe.

Yeah, Riley was not going to mind her own business.

"I know you don't really like Derek," Lucy said.

Riley shook her head. "It's not that I don't like him. I don't think he's the right guy for you though."

"But you *don't* like him."

Riley blew out a breath and thought about that. "He just… drives me nuts," she said. "It's not really dislike."

Derek had always been around. She couldn't remember a single significant event in her brother's life when Derek hadn't also been there. So she'd experienced the naughty-little-boy side of him, complete with spiders in her bedroom and hiding in closets to scare her. She'd experienced the annoying-teenager side of him, when he and Kyle would raid the kitchen and eat all of *her* cereal, or when they'd blast the music while she was trying to study, or when they'd kick her out of the basement—her haven—so they could hang out with their friends… and debase her couch. She'd experienced the idiotic-young-adult side too. When he and Kyle would drink too much and pass out at her house—once on her bedroom floor for some reason that neither of them had ever been able to explain—or when Kyle would come home from college and they'd stay up all night…again in *her* basement.

He was always around. And not just for Kyle's stuff. He'd been at every one of *her* birthday parties, the one time she'd gone to the Homecoming dance, and her graduation. Significant moments in her life and he'd been there like he had every right.

He just annoyed her. She couldn't put her finger on it exactly.

But she *could* put her finger on why she didn't want Derek dating Lucy. "He's messing around, Luce. He thinks he wants to date a nice girl, someone different from his usual, but he's never done that before and I'm afraid that...he won't like it." She shrugged. She didn't think Lucy would actually take offense at that. "He doesn't really know what a real relationship looks like. With a woman," she added. Because she had to give him credit. He knew how to be a good friend, a good son, a good employee, and a good citizen. "I just don't want anyone I care about getting hurt because Derek is feeling restless."

She frowned. Derek *should* be able to have a good relationship with a woman. And really, if he was talking about trying something serious with a woman who had been in other relationships and had some experience, it would be okay. It wouldn't hurt him to be in a real relationship where they talked and did things together that didn't involve, well, any panties on any floors.

And why did she feel a little like she was blushing, thinking of the way he'd said the word "panties"? *That* was ridiculous. She took a sip of the cocoa.

And damn. That was good. So Derek was a Cocoa God too?

Finally Lucy nodded. "That makes sense."

"It does?" Riley *wanted* it to. She didn't want anyone getting their hearts broken, but she also didn't want to sound like some kind of lunatic who thought she should get to say who did and didn't date Derek. Even if she told herself she was doing a good deed for the nice women of Sapphire Falls, she realized that her concern was actually a by-product of two things—the fact that she knew Derek too well and couldn't quite forget what an idiot he'd been over the years, and the fact that she had way too much time on her hands to sit around thinking about all of this.

"Sure," Lucy said, with a nod. "He likes the *idea* of a relationship, but he doesn't understand the reality. And I wouldn't be a good person to teach him about dating."

"You wouldn't?" Riley thought, on one hand, that Lucy could teach Derek a lot about class and sincerity and, well, stuff that didn't have anything to do with panties.

Lucy gave her a small smile. "I don't know much about dating myself. How could I teach him?"

Teach him.

Yeah. That's actually what Derek needed. Someone to teach him. To try out dating a nice girl, he'd have to, well, date a nice girl. And that nice girl would then be at risk for heartbreak. Riley didn't really want *any* nice girl going through that. But *someone* needed to show him what it was like.

She looked over at Derek. Then back to Lucy. Then back to Derek again. He was laughing at something Mitch Dugan, the contractor working on expanding the Come Again with pizza ovens, had just said. She suddenly flashed back to many other times when he'd laughed. And made those around him laugh. It was a regular thing.

And he looked good doing it.

"So you're not interested in Derek?" Riley asked Lucy flat out.

Lucy shook her head with a soft laugh. "I like Derek. I appreciate all of his help all the time. But I don't think Derek and I have much in common."

Okay, so that made this easier. Lucy wasn't interested in dating Derek. But Derek thought he was interested in dating Lucy. There was really only one thing Riley could do here. At least now that she'd convinced herself that the honorable thing to do would be to keep Derek from breaking *any* nice-girl hearts. Honorable was good.

Torturing Derek Wright a little was too.

"Hey, I'll be right back," she told Lucy, shoving her chair back and standing before she could think better of her plan.

"Okay. I'll get everything pulled up." Lucy shifted forward in her chair and reached for Riley's laptop.

Riley was using her master's degree in computer science to update various websites for people in Sapphire Falls. It was slowly killing her. But at least it was something to do.

And hey, reforming Derek Wright was also, if nothing else, something to do.

————

"I need to talk to you."

Derek turned as Riley walked up, grabbed the sleeve of his shirt, and started for the kitchen.

She was damned bossy. "Uh, I'm kind of talking to Mitch," Derek pointed out. They were talking about whether jalapeno peppers ever belonged on pizza, but still.

She didn't stop walking...or dragging him along.

"*What*?" he asked when the kitchen door had swung shut behind him.

She dropped her hold on him and turned, crossing her arms. She watched him for a moment, and he felt how a used car might feel when someone was taking their first good look.

"I have an idea."

He felt a definite sense of trepidation at those four words. But trepidation had never held him back before. "About what?"

"You becoming a better guy."

He lifted his eyebrows.

"Or, more specifically, you deserving to date nice girls. Like Lucy."

"I have to *deserve* it?"

"Yes." She didn't even hesitate a second.

"So you're going to test me or something?"

"Nope. I'm going to *train* you."

He felt his eyes widen. "Excuse me?"

She nodded. "Seriously. You need to try out an actual *relationship* before you get into one with a nice girl, realize you hate it, and break somebody's heart."

"And you're going to teach me?"

But that didn't sound quite as crazy as it should have. He really didn't know how to date a nice girl for real. He knew how to make a woman laugh. How to help her forget her troubles. How to feel more confident. But he ran the show in those situations. They were short-term. He didn't really know how to do the two-way thing, or even what was expected of him in a relationship like that. Riley was Lucy's best friend. She probably could teach him a thing or two. But...

"That means *we're* going to have to spend a bunch of time together, huh?"

She narrowed her eyes but nodded.

It was stupid. He annoyed Riley more than anyone. And vice versa. And yet, he didn't mind the idea of hanging out with her. With Riley, there was never a dull moment. He could tease her without worrying about hurting her feelings. He wouldn't have to be perfect. She'd tell him he was being dick, but she wouldn't get all hung up on it. She'd be that bratty little sister she'd always been. Riley would not only be able to tell him what nice girls expected, but she sure as hell would call him out when he got it wrong.

It all sunk in a lot faster than he would have expected. "This might work."

She looked a little surprised. "Really?"

He laughed. "Yeah, it's a good idea. You can show me what it's like to date a nice girl and nobody gets hurt."

"And I get to say when you're ready to ask someone out. *If* you ever get ready."

Yeah, yeah, he was going to have to play by Riley's rules. He could do that. How hard could it really be to date a nice girl? "Fine. So when do we start?"

She gave him a grin and stuck out her hand. "Right now."

He looked down at her hand, then back up.

He'd never shaken hands with a hot woman that he was going to date. Even if it was kind of fake dating.

Of course, he'd never really *dated* anyone since high school. He shrugged and took her hand. What the hell? Might as well start doing everything differently right now.

Riley stared into her bathroom mirror the next morning. It was seven a.m. As in five hours after she'd gone to bed. She should not be up.

But her mother was up. And making waffles. Which was, without a doubt, the loudest breakfast someone could make. Besides the banging of pots and pans, there was also the TODAY show blasting from the television that sat on the counter next to the mixer so her mom could hear it over the sound of the mixer itself—because apparently you couldn't mix waffle batter by hand—and the horrible, piercing beeping of the waffle iron every time a waffle was done cooking.

Riley scrubbed a hand over her face and looked into her bloodshot eyes. Yeah, it was going to be a long day.

"Riley! I'm making breakfast!"

No shit. "Yeah! Coming!" She didn't want waffles. But she wanted coffee. And lots of it. And that was upstairs with the waffles. And her parents. *Kill me now.*

She really needed to get a job. In California. Far from Sapphire Falls. She'd gone into computer science because it had seemed less personal, frankly, than a lot of jobs. Jobs like becoming a doctor. More specifically, *the* doctor for her small hometown. Kyle, had known what he wanted to do with his life since he was about eight years old. And it had always involved staying in Sapphire Falls.

Riley had been the opposite. She hadn't known what she wanted to do until she'd taken a computer class her junior year of high school. And even then, it had simply been something she liked and was good at. It wasn't like she had a *passion* for it. They were just machines. The jobs in cyber security paid well and they were far from Sapphire Falls. And being in cyber security sounded better to her mother than gamer-girl. Which she also was. She just hadn't figured out how to make a living doing that.

Of course, getting tossed in jail—even if her name had been cleared later—for her cyber security job hadn't sat well with her mother. Or her employment prospects.

Which meant she was jobless and homeless and on her way to penniless. For now. Temporarily. It *had to be* temporary. She simply couldn't tolerate anything else. She could design websites. She could start a podcast about her favorite video game. If prepubescent boys could make good money doing that, she surely could. She could design her own video game. She knew nothing about marketing that or...really anything else that had anything to do with starting a business like that, but she could definitely design her own game. And it would be kick-ass.

"Riley! The bacon is getting cold!"

Riley blew out a breath. Sure. She *could* do all of that. But she needed to move out of her parents' house yesterday. Because living in her parents' basement and spending most of her time on her computer was pathetic and way too much like how she'd spent ages twelve to eighteen.

"Riley!"

Oh yeah, and it was annoying.

She combed her fingers through her hair, cinched the belt on her robe tighter, and took a deep breath. Then made the climb to the kitchen.

"I can't believe they're raising that much money for a *prom*," Erika Ames was saying to her husband.

Riley's dad, Jake, nodded. "It goes up every year."

"But twelve thousand dollars? For a *party*?" Erika asked, transferring bacon from the skillet to a plate.

Riley crossed to the cupboard that housed the coffee cups. See, there was no way the bacon was getting cold. Her mom had *just* taken it out of the pan. Riley sighed.

"That's scandalous," Erika said. "The food bank could use that money. The senior center. The daycare."

Riley filled her cup with coffee that she knew would be nice and strong. Thankfully, that was one thing she and her father agreed on. But as she turned and leaned back against the counter, taking that first sip, she had to admit that it wasn't really her dad she had a hard time agreeing with. Her dad was a pretty laid-back guy.

Her mom on the other hand was...Kyle. Or rather, she was where Kyle got his do-gooder-save-the-world side. Not that Riley was a complete loser bitch. But she wasn't the Boy Scout her brother was.

"That's a lot of money," Jake agreed, turning the page on the newspaper he held.

"You don't think they should do something more important with it?" Erika asked. She stabbed a fork into a waffle and flopped it onto Jake's plate.

Jake folded the paper down and eyed the waffle, then looked up at his wife of thirty-two years. "I think the kids will make some great memories in a safe and fun environment with that money, and I think that's important."

Erika's shoulders relaxed a little and she gave him a smile. "You're right, I suppose. It would be nice if they could do it for less, but that's not the most terrible thing in the world."

Jake nodded and reached for the syrup.

While Erika started in on something else. Something about

the garden and some bugs that were eating her roses, and then Jake said something about picking up something at the gardening store in York when he went over later, and again Erika settled. It was mostly blah, blah, blah to Riley, but while she wasn't listening to the words, she was watching her parents.

Maybe for the first time.

It was strange. All of this was how it had always been. Erika got worked up and emotional and Jake settled her down. Riley had seen that exact thing over and over in her life, but she'd never really thought about it. Now, for some reason, she found herself studying it.

It was so...normal. Her mom and dad just fit together. Sure, some of it was habit. After that long together, how could it not be? But you had to stick around with someone to establish habits. Erika and Jake Ames fit. They balanced each other.

Riley had always found that very boring. Very predictable. Her parents had met when Erika had been a sophomore in high school and Jake was a senior. They'd dated, gotten engaged, then married, then had two kids. Exactly the way everyone else in Sapphire Falls did.

That was another reason Riley had gotten out of town. It seemed that this tendency to just go along with tradition was in the water, and she was afraid to drink too much of it.

"Riley?"

She shook herself and focused on her mother. It seemed that Erika had been trying to get her attention. "Um, yeah?"

"How many waffles do you want?"

A flutter of panic rippled through her chest. For some reason, those waffles felt symbolic in that moment. She couldn't eat the same waffles made in the same waffle iron in the same kitchen that she'd been eating all her life. She needed more. Different. And if she took a bite of those waffles, and they were amazing and comforting, then she might decide that they were good enough, and that eating them for the rest of her life wasn't the worst thing that could ever happen...

"I have to go," she said quickly.

Her mother's eyes widened. No one, in her experience, walked out on waffles.

"Where? Now?"

"Yes. *Right now*." She probably didn't need to emphasize that quite so firmly.

"But..." Erika looked toward the waffle iron, then over to her husband.

Jake was watching them, seeming curious as well. But he was still chewing.

"The waffles," Erika finally finished, as if she truly was speechless at the idea of someone *not* wanting her waffles.

"I know. But I have to be somewhere." Where, she wasn't sure, but she'd figure that out after she was out of this house. This place that was comforting and cramped at the same time. Yes, she felt pathetic about moving back home and now living her own version of *Groundhog Day*—a fabulous and horrifying movie. What she'd done for the past week, okay month, was pretty much what she'd done all the weeks of her summer vacations at age fourteen. With the exception of hanging out at the Come Again.

Which brought Derek to mind. And the other thing she had definitely *not* done in high school—giving someone advice about relationships.

Yeah, for all her rebellious tats and piercings and black clothing and hair dye, she hadn't known crap about anything other than video games and exasperating her mother.

She was pretty much full circle here.

Except that Derek Wright wanted her to make him a better man.

She could do that. She had to do that. Because the alternative was waffles with her parents and—

"Good morning!"

Riley groaned internally. Waffles with her parents and her perfect, life-on-track brother.

"Hi, everyone."

And his perfect, shit-together fiancée, Hannah.

"Good morning!" Erika was clearly relieved that *someone* was going to be eating waffles and bacon since Riley was letting her down.

Was she rebelling against waffles? Fuck yeah, she was. And normalcy and clichés and following in the perfect footsteps in front of her.

Why?

Well...because she always had. And she was happy. And... yeah, that's all she had.

She escaped the kitchen and headed downstairs to get dressed. Okay, another difference in living at home compared to high school was that her bedroom had not been in the basement when she was a teen. She'd slept upstairs. In a room that was yellow and lavender. Now she was in the basement, where she had her own bathroom and living area and...that was it. This sucked.

She got dressed, pulled her hair up into a bun, washed her face and brushed her teeth and was back upstairs within fifteen minutes. "Bye!"

"Will you be home for supper?" Erika called to her from the kitchen table, where she was happily seated with her husband, son, and future daughter-in-law in the most normal, most cliché, most all-across-Sapphire-Falls-at-this-very-moment way. They were, of course, drinking coffee and eating the waffles. The delicious, I-can-easily-trick-you-into-feeling-like-this-is-enough-forever waffles.

Riley gripped the door handle tightly, so desperately wanting to say that no, she would not be home for supper. But where was she going to be? "Yeah. I'll see you later."

"Cheesy chicken and broccoli casserole," Erika said with a big smile.

Riley groaned and pulled the door shut firmly behind her.

Her mother's cheesy chicken and broccoli casserole was amazing. Climbing those basement stairs to eat that once a week for the rest of her life wouldn't be *horrible*.

Fuck.

4

———

"**A**lright! For fuck's sake!" Derek yanked his front door open and stood staring—with a mix of surprise, trepidation, and concern—at Riley Ames.

"Morning!" She gave him a big, almost perky smile.

Except that Riley was never what he'd call perky.

"Are you okay?" He was aware that he was scowling. But fuck, it was *early*.

Her smile dropped and she frowned. "Yes. Why?"

"It's not even eight a.m."

Her perkiness slipped a bit and she sighed. "I know, right?"

"So what's going on?"

"I'm here to have breakfast with you."

Now his brows lifted. "Why?"

"Because that's something that happens in normal, not-just-fucking-around relationships."

Ah. Wonderful. His training was starting. At the crack of dawn. Okay, to be fair, the sun had been up for a couple of hours, but this was way before he normally rolled out of bed. Riley too. He narrowed his eyes. "You're not a morning person."

She shrugged. "But your future sweet, contributes-to-society-with-a-real-job girlfriend might be."

"Is Lucy a morning person?"

She didn't roll her eyes, but it seemed that she wanted to. "She is, actually. She does yoga and then reads the paper while she drinks her coffee."

Hmm, yoga. He realized Riley was dressed in a pair of yoga pants, as a matter of fact, and a tank top. Her hair was in a messy knot on top of her head and she was wearing glasses.

She looked really hot in those glasses.

He blinked.

What? He'd just thought of Riley as hot? It wasn't technically the first time. She *was* hot. It was just a fact. And he'd realized it and acknowledged in the same way he acknowledged a sunny, 70-degree day. It was something that was a fact and was happening around him, but that didn't really affect anything.

It was different this time. It seemed that Riley *was* affecting him. That was...weird. And probably complicated. But mostly weird.

He'd seen her dressed like this before. Fitted clothes that hugged her body and showed off her tats and piercings and smooth, creamy skin, and curves—

Wait. No, he hadn't. He'd appreciated her tats and piercings and the streaks of color she put in her hair and the dramatic makeup she seemed to prefer, because it was so funny that she looked nothing like the nerdy, bookworm gamer-girl she was. But he'd never thought of her skin as *creamy*.

"Are you here to do yoga?" Did his voice sound funny?

Riley tipped her head. "I'm more of a kick-boxing girl."

He snorted. That didn't surprise him at all. "I'm just saying, if I have to get up early, seeing a bendy girl in skimpy clothes seems like an okay perk." *Seeing you bending over would be a perk.*

Fuck. He couldn't be thinking things like that. This was Riley. She was not only Kyle's little sister, but she found Derek incredibly irritating. Oh, and she was here to teach him how to date another woman.

"You can't sit an ogle a woman while she does yoga," Riley said.

He sure as hell could. "So what should I do while she does yoga?"

"Make her French-press coffee. And crepes. And go out back and pick her some flowers for the breakfast table. And put her towel in the dryer so it's warm after her shower."

Derek blinked at her again. That was all very specific. And...romantic. How did Riley know this stuff? Had some guy done those things for her? And who was he?

And why in the hell did Derek feel a prick of annoyance behind his breastbone at the idea of her wrapping up in a towel some guy had warmed for her?

"You're going to teach me to be romantic then?" he asked. "That's what nice girls like?"

"*All* girls like that."

"*A lot* of girls would like me to bend them over on their yoga mat." Like almost all of the girls he usually hung out with.

Had he said that to put a sexual image in Riley's head? Hell yes, he had. Why? Well, that was the real question. Riley didn't like him. What good did it do to put sexual thoughts in her head? Of course, her not liking him was kind of why he did most of the things he did when she was around. Pushing her buttons was just so damned fun.

But Riley didn't blush or act surprised or offended at his comment. She lifted her chin and said, "And if there were flowers and crepes on the breakfast table afterward, I guarantee your chances of getting a before-work blowjob would increase exponentially."

Riley Ames had just said the word blowjob to him.

Derek wasn't sure what to do with that. He might have vaguely registered her hotness before, but he knew for a fact she'd never said the words blow and job together like that to him before.

As he was still trying to unstick his tongue from the roof of his mouth, she moved to push past him, and her bare shoulder brushed over his bare sternum. Derek became acutely aware that he was in only the pair of gym shorts that he'd pulled on when the pounding had erupted from his front door.

It seemed the same realization hit her at the same moment. They both froze, both holding their breaths.

It wasn't like they hadn't been in tight quarters before. Surely they'd passed close to one another in a hallway or had to move around one another in a small space at some point in the twenty-six years he'd known her.

But if he'd ever been hit in the gut by how soft and warm her skin was or how great her hair smelled, he'd promptly forgotten it. He'd never felt an urge to lean in and take a big breath. And maybe drag his mouth up and down her throat.

Until *this* moment, anyway.

Because yeah, her hair fucking smelled amazing, and she *was* very warm and soft.

Slowly—very slowly—she turned toward him. Her shoulder grazing his chest again. Her eyes lifted to his, taking time to track over his pecs, shoulders, throat and mouth before making eye contact, however. She swallowed.

"But I'm going to make *you* crepes today."

Yeah, *her* voice definitely sounded funny.

"Do I like crepes?" And did that mean she was romancing him? Well, no. She was just going through the motions of romance so he'd learn.

"If you don't, you will," she told him with a little cockiness in her voice that was so familiar and yet, also sent a bolt of heat through him.

"That's pretty big talk." He was more a bacon-and-eggs kind of guy. And he had no idea what French-press coffee was.

"Well, this isn't actually about what *you* like," she told him. They were still standing really close. She'd turned enough that they were no longer touching, but the centimeters of space between them were full of heat.

"Right. So Lucy likes crepes," Derek said.

Something flickered in Riley's eyes but after a moment, she nodded. "Yes. She does. And cream in her coffee."

He should make a note of that. But all he could think was that Riley drank her coffee black.

Finally, Riley stepped the rest of the way through the door and headed for his kitchen. With the bag from the grocery store that he had just now noticed.

He blew out a breath and followed her.

"And put a shirt on," she called over her shoulder.

"Why?"

"Because you walking around half-naked would make Lucy uncomfortable."

"Lucy's not here." But he snagged a clean T-shirt from the basket of clothes he'd left on the sofa.

"You need to practice what it will be like when she is," Riley said. "You might spend the majority of your time with women half-naked, but you need to do things differently with a real girlfriend."

He stepped into the kitchen, still just holding his shirt. Why? Because he kind of enjoyed making Riley uncomfortable? But she didn't seem uncomfortable exactly. She did seem a little jumpy though. Like she was trying to avoid looking at him. Which automatically made him want her even jumpier.

He crossed the kitchen floor to get closer to her. He couldn't explain it other than to say that there had never been a time he could remember, from the time she was a little girl to now, that he'd been around Riley Ames and *hadn't* wanted to get her attention. Even if it was negative attention.

He'd always chalked it up to their like-a-brother-and-sister relationship. But he was absolutely questioning everything about that right now. Because her nipples were pressing against the front of her tank top, and he loved *that* reaction more than any other he'd ever gotten out of her.

"Seems like I might spend even *more* time without clothes on with a real girlfriend," he said.

Riley spun away as he got closer and started pulling items out of the grocery bag. "You have to do normal things with a real girlfriend," she said. "And most normal things require clothes."

"Normal things like what?" He watched her set flour, sugar, eggs, and milk on the counter. She didn't think he'd have those things? But then he thought about it. He wasn't sure he did have flour.

"Things like..." She trailed off and gave an exasperated sigh, then turned, seeming reluctant. "You can't have sex with a woman every single time you're alone together."

"Why not?"

"Because you have to get to *know* her. You have to *talk*. You have to do things together like make meals, and watch TV and movies, and talk about pop culture and politics and current events. That's how you learn about what kind of person she is and what she likes and doesn't like. Otherwise, you won't really know if you like being together or not, and if you should keep seeing her or not."

Yep, that made sense.

"Okay." He pulled his shirt over his head. "But the physical stuff is important too."

"I think you've practiced *that* plenty." Riley turned away and started opening his cupboards and drawers.

He would help her find whatever she was looking for, but first he wanted to finish this subject. "But we have to be comfortable together physically," he said.

She turned back to face him quickly. "We do?"

"We...as in me and my real girlfriend," he said, but his thoughts were on all of the times he and Riley had been together in swimming suits and pajamas, when he'd had his shirt off, when she'd gotten soaked with water balloons and her white T-shirt had been plastered to her body, when she'd pulled off a tank top and replaced it with a T-shirt in the back of Kyle's car. He remembered thinking, "Hey, Riley has boobs," when he'd glanced over his shoulder and caught a glimpse of her pale pink bra. But it had been only a few seconds. And it had been Riley. It hadn't mattered.

She'd slept in a tiny tent with him and Kyle while camping. She'd swum in the pond with them. She'd leaned her head on his shoulder in the backseat and slept all the way home from a Dierks Bentley concert in Lawrence, Kansas. He'd thrown her over his shoulder and carried her out of a party at Damon Jenkins's house when she'd gotten puking drunk and started telling Carrie Reynolds what she really thought of her.

Yeah, they'd been physically close and not-fully-dressed several times together. And yet, *now* she seemed jumpy. And he couldn't really focus on the fact they were talking about another woman together.

"I get that it has to be more than physical," he said, his thoughts still scattered. "But it has to be physical *too*."

Riley took a deep breath and nodded. "Yeah. Of course. There has to be physical attraction too. And you have to want to be close to each other, touching, stuff like that."

"So, seems like Lucy might need to get comfortable with the physical side." His eyes flickered to Riley's mouth, and he felt a stab of surprise and desire at the same time. "Cooking breakfast and talking about current events while also touching and being half-naked."

He'd really like to pull the strap of her tank top down her shoulder and kiss her right there.

The thought occurred to him and didn't shock him as much

as it should have. Especially considering they were talking about him doing all of this with one of her best friends.

Riley gave him a frown. "Really? Already?"

"Already what?"

"You're already changing the rules. You can't get through one morning without wondering how to do things *your* way instead of hers?"

He opened his mouth. Then snapped it shut. Dammit. The thing was, he hadn't really been thinking about Lucy. If she was more shy and would take longer to warm up, of course he'd take it slower. Not make their first breakfast together half-naked. But he hadn't been thinking about Lucy.

Still, she had a point. "Okay, okay." He looked at the table where they'd be eating. Fine. He could be taught. He headed for the backyard and returned five minutes later with a handful of the rhubarb that grew along his back fence.

Riley watched him grab a plastic cup from The Stop, the convenience store on the edge of town, and stick the stalks inside. He set them in the middle of the table.

She was clearly fighting a smile when he turned to face her.

"I don't have flowers. That and green beans and tomatoes are what grow in my backyard, and I know how you feel about green beans."

Her eyes widened. "What?"

"You don't like green beans straight from the garden. But you do like rhubarb. I mean, maybe not raw, but..." He shrugged. "You're not really a flower kind of girl."

Her eyes got even rounder. "I'm not?"

She wasn't. He wasn't going to be able to give her a rundown of all the reasons he thought that—for instance, she never wore flowered patterns on her clothes—but honestly, even if he'd been driving her crazy for twenty-six years, he knew her. Period. He wasn't going to fight with her about it. "You're not," he said simply.

"But this is about Lucy."

"Yeah, well, Lucy isn't here right now."

They just stood looking at each other for several long seconds.

Then Riley nodded. "Well, I didn't do any bendy yoga, so I guess all of this is just as close as we can get today. But that's why you're practicing."

"So I need to plant flowers?"

"I don't...that seems...a little more involved than it needs to be," she said after tripping over the first few words.

Yeah, maybe. Which also maybe meant that he should do it. This was about doing things differently. But that seemed kind of—well, not permanent, because flowers weren't, of course, but they lasted longer than his relationships typically did. Yeah, maybe he should plant some flowers.

"What kind?"

"Of flowers to plant?"

"Yeah."

"I'll, um, ask Lucy what she likes," Riley said.

"What kind of flowers does your grandma like?" he asked.

Riley looked surprised. "My grandma?"

Riley's grandmother and Derek's were best friends. He knew Ruby as well as he did his own. And loved her just as much. "Yeah. My grandma loves lilacs."

"Mine does too. And roses, of course."

"I could plant roses."

"Roses are kind of hard to grow."

He shrugged. "I'm pretty good with plants."

"Why are you planting flowers our grandmothers like?" Riley crossed her arms.

"Because if the relationship thing doesn't work out, then I've still got someone to give the flowers to."

Riley didn't say anything to that at first. She studied him for a moment. He lifted a brow. Finally, she said, "Grandma loves

Butterfly Weed. And the butterflies and hummingbirds it attracts. And it's easy to grow."

"Great. Perfect."

Riley shook her head.

"What?" he asked.

"That's very sweet."

"Is it?"

"Of course." She laughed and dropped her arms. "You don't know that?"

"So being romantic is really just doing thoughtful things," he said.

"Yeah, pretty much."

"Then this will be easy. I'm a very thoughtful guy."

She snorted at that. And he realized that yeah, she would snort. He *was* very thoughtful. To everyone but Riley. Because he wanted people to be happy and feel good. He wanted Riley wound up.

That realization seemed to hit him right between the eyes.

It wasn't that he didn't want her *happy*. But while he spent his time making the town a better place, making people's lives a little easier, with Riley, it was different. He liked to give her a hard time and get her going. Why was that? Why was she the one spot he wanted worked up in his otherwise peaceful, relatively carefree life?

That was...interesting.

"You realize that having multiple types of coffee creamer for your overnight guests' morning coffee is also sweet, right?" Riley asked.

He frowned. "How did you know about that?"

"The girls in the bar that first night," she said.

Damn, those girls had spilled a lot.

"The whole idea is making them feel better about...whatever. And saying goodbye in the morning can be awkward. The coffee makes it better."

Riley nodded, still watching him as if she was pondering something serious. "That's all you really need to do, you know," she finally said.

"What do you mean?"

"You just have to think about how to make her feel good, make her happy."

He shifted his weight. Yeah, he got that.

"And you already do that," Riley pointed out.

"Yes, but the orgasms the night before make the coffee taste even better."

She didn't fall for him trying to lighten things. "You do understand this."

Of course he did. He wasn't an idiot. No, he was just cursed with a deeply engrained desire to make things better around him. To make things work better, to make people feel better, to even make things *look* better. The fucking town square's landscaping was a testament to that. But he also had an allergy to clinginess. He wanted to do things for people because he wanted to, not because they *needed* him to or expected him to.

Honestly, with his parents, there was really no other way he could have turned out. His father was involved in everything from planning the town's Fourth of July display to serving on the school board. And his mom didn't trust his dad any further than she could throw him. She inundated him with texts all day and peppered him with questions as soon as he set foot through the door.

So Derek had learned to balance wanting to take care of things with his absolute unwillingness to have someone on his ass constantly. He made women feel good—beautiful and desirable—he made them laugh, he was sweet to them. Then he got them out of his house and life before they could even begin to think they might have a right to know where he was going to spend his *next* weekend. A reputation for one-weekend stands and coffee to go had served him well. Those little creamer tubs and to-go cups were the best, most symbolic things he could have bought. *I care that you have your coffee exactly the way you want it* combined with *I wouldn't want you to spill it while you're driving* away *from my house.*

"Making a woman happy between the sheets is easy, and then all I have to do is get through coffee," he said. "That's not really that much of a challenge."

"So what you need to practice is doing the sweet thing longer term."

"Guess so." And risk the clingy thing. Dammit. He knew that would come. It was unavoidable. A "real" girlfriend, as they'd been referring to Lucy, would come to depend on him. But maybe it was time. Scott and Kyle seemed to be doing okay. Derek would just ignore the cold sweats the idea gave him.

"And you need to practice keeping your clothes on the whole time you're with someone."

"The *whole* time?" And his thoughts were right back on Riley again and how *clingy* her clothes were.

Or had his thoughts ever really *left* Riley? Because he'd just been kind of wondering what he could substitute for the morning-coffee-creamer thing for a woman who didn't use coffee creamer.

But it wasn't hard to *imagine* her without clothes. Her nipples would probably be pale pink to go with her pale skin. And she seemed the type to shave *everywhere*. He wasn't at all sure why he thought that, but yeah, he really would put money down on Riley being bare. And she might have some hidden tats.

And he suddenly wanted to know *all* of that.

"What the hell, Derek?" she asked, snapping her fingers in front of him.

"What?"

"Are you actually thinking about *me* without clothes on?"

How the hell did she know that? "It just kind of happened," he admitted.

"But I'm like a sister to you. *Right*?"

She said the last word as if she would take no other answer. And the answer should be easy. It was yes. Absolutely. Up until about twenty minutes ago.

"It's just a reflex," he said, frowning. "Calm down."

Was it so horrible that he might think about her as more than a sister? But yeah, to her, probably. He was just a pain-in-the-ass guy who'd been in her way forever and who had never gotten his shit together enough to even leave home.

And what the *hell* was *that*?

Riley Ames was *not* going to make him feel like a loser. Plenty of women thought he was damned amazing. God level, in fact. Yeah, he fucking loved that. And loved that she knew that. He wasn't saving lives like Kyle or protecting the town like Scott, but he was making people here happier. Mostly female people, sure, but when they felt better about themselves, the people around them benefitted. It was a proven psychological fact that people were more productive and nicer to the people they interacted with when they felt good. Great sex was like eating healthy and working out and vacation. He was like their trainer.

He still lived in his hometown and there was nothing fucking wrong with that. No matter what Riley thought. She was the *least* clingy person he knew. She didn't even cling to fond childhood memories or the idea of being in her hometown every year at Christmas. *Some* clinginess wasn't all bad.

"Are we cooking or what?" he asked crossly.

He was hungry. And up early. And turned on by a woman who was off-limits. And who he didn't really like that much anyway.

The least he could get was a good breakfast.

———

S he was making crepes with Derek Wright. How had that happened?

"That one's the best yet." He slid the last crepe onto the plate and handed it to her. "Now what?"

Riley narrowed her eyes. This was nice. He wasn't giving her a hard time. He wasn't messing around. He was following her directions and making crepes that were turning out to be really good.

"Blueberry pomegranate chai seed jam," she said, reaching for the jar in the sack she'd brought in with her. "I roll it all inside, but you can put it on top if you want."

"Okay. Sounds good."

It did?

He wasn't going to tease her about her not-plain-old-strawberry jam? He wasn't going to give her a hard time about the chai seeds?

That was nice. And weird.

It was like he was lost in thought or distracted or something. Or maybe it was like he was being normal. How he was with other people. Not her, of course. Derek was never *not* messing around and not giving her a hard time. But she assumed he was normal and not irritating at least some of the time with other people. He seemed to be well-liked.

She spooned jam onto the crepes and Derek rolled them up. Then she dolloped whipped cream on top, and he took the plates over to the table. She frowned at his back.

But this was definitely not how he usually acted with her. Hell, the last time they'd been alone in a kitchen together, he'd started a food fight.

Her mother had been *pissed*. Until Derek teased her and got her laughing and charmed her right out of her bad mood.

Yeah, Derek was going to be fine at this relationships stuff.

He was wonderful with her mother, their grandmothers…hell, he was sweet to the entire town of Sapphire Falls. He basically romanced the town all the time. He'd just never applied it to a woman.

The thing was, once he decided to, he'd probably be really good at it.

How had she not seen that? She hadn't thought it through. Because with *her*, he was a…pain in the ass. He liked to push her buttons and tease. And not in a sexy way. In a…well, a pushing-her-buttons kind of way. He was different with her, but yeah, he kind of had some potential for being boyfriend material after all. Maybe there was a chance he could pull it off.

Like a 40% chance.

But that wasn't good enough for girls like Lucy. No, Riley wasn't *actually* training him to be the perfect boyfriend for Lucy. Lucy wasn't interested. But Derek didn't know that and it was fun to lead him on, letting him think that Riley was hauling him out of bed before his alarm because Lucy was a morning person, when really Riley just wanted to mess with him a little. She owed him for the ants in her peanut butter. At least. Anyone would agree. And she wanted to test him. Test him to see just how far he'd go to become a "better man" for these sweet, nice girls he thought he wanted to date.

Riley poured coffee and carried the cups to the table. She drank it black and so did Derek. In spite of the multitude of cream flavors he kept around.

"You okay?" she asked as she slid into the chair perpendicular to him.

He cut into one of the crepes. "Yeah." He lifted it to his mouth. He tasted the bite, chewing slowly. Then he nodded. "This is really good."

"Thanks." She sipped her coffee.

He sipped his coffee.

She took a bite of her crepe. Which was really good.

He took another bite.

She took another sip of coffee. And tried not to grind her teeth.

At her parents' house, she would give a hundred bucks every morning just to sit at the table and eat without conversation. But with Derek, this felt awkward.

"I don't think I've ever had anything that was blueberry and pomegranate together," he said, taking another bite.

She blinked at him, waiting for him to make some disparaging comment about pomegranates. She didn't really know how someone would disparage pomegranates, but Derek would find a way. Even if he didn't mean it. She knew, had always known, that about 70% of the stuff he gave her shit about was just to give her shit and wasn't actually how he felt.

When she'd gone through the phase where she'd studied and listened to everything the Beatles had ever done, Derek had delighted in telling her "behind the scenes" stories about the guys. About 90% of what he'd told her was complete bullshit. Just like the things he'd told her he'd read about the dangers of a vegan diet when she'd gone through that phase had been 90% bullshit. Just like the statistics he'd cited when they'd argued about the government's climate change policies had been 90% bullshit. Just like most of the things they'd ever argued about had been around 92% bullshit on his part. He just seemed incapable of agreeing with her and having the conversation end cordially.

All of which made her conscience completely clear about her fake nice-guy training program.

And maybe it wasn't *entirely* fake. If he warmed up a towel for a woman while she was in the shower, even once ever, Riley would have done a very good deed.

But Derek said nothing disparaging about pomegranates. He just took another bite.

Riley slapped her hand down on the table. "What are you doing?"

He cocked an eyebrow. "Eating."

"You're eating *crepes*," she said. "With blueberry pomegranate *chai seed* jam."

He cut off another piece. "I know."

"And you haven't said one thing about how the chai seed farmers are slowly poisoning us with pesticides, or asking if eating crepes will suddenly give you the urge to go see a musical."

He chewed, watching her. After he swallowed, he took a sip of coffee. "No, I haven't," he finally agreed.

"Why not?"

"Because..."

She frowned as he trailed off. "Because why?"

"Because I wouldn't say any of that to Lucy."

It was the dumbest thing...but Riley felt a little prick of annoyance at that. She should *want* him to be nice. She didn't want him to tease her about crepes and chai seeds. She wanted him to practice just hanging out with a woman. She wanted to see him being a normal, nice guy since as far as she knew, that side of him was theoretic.

But now that he was doing it, she was annoyed.

"Well, stop it, it's creepy when it's you and me," she said, cutting into her own crepe with a scowl.

"It's creepy for me to be nice?" he asked.

"It's just not...you," she said, scowling harder as she concentrated on the crepe. Or at least on spreading the blueish-purple jam around her plate.

"I don't have breakfast with women I'm not related to," he said.

"You've had breakfast with me before." She wasn't sure why she felt the need to point that out. She knew she was being contrary. She was trying to teach him to be nice and sweet, and now he was being nice and sweet and she was trying to get him to stop. But...it felt wrong. Fake. Like he was trying too hard. And she realized that things with her and Derek had always been pretty easy. And honest.

"I have." He took a breath. "I don't have breakfast with women I don't know really well. And I don't watch my mouth with women I have breakfast with."

And that, stupidly, made her feel warmer. He did know her well. Maybe better than she'd ever realized. That also made her feel strangely restless.

"So I'm practicing, I guess."

Riley watched him frown and realized that he was uncomfortable too. Okay, *that* was weird. One, Derek Wright was never uncomfortable. He made situations comfortable for other people. That was almost his entire purpose in life. Two, this was *her*. He should not be uncomfortable around her. And vice versa.

She set her fork down. "Well, it's creepy," she said.

He sighed.

"Listen, I think you can practice hanging out with someone, fully clothed, doing things other than...fornicating..."

He snorted at that and she smiled. Okay, that was good.

"And still be yourself," she finished. "In fact, I mean... you *should* be yourself. Just, you know, with your clothes on."

"You keep making that point."

"I think it's an important one to keep at the forefront."

He smiled, and she felt herself relax.

"I can't treat other girls the way I treat you," he said.

She didn't know why, but her heart sped up. "You can't?"

"You're...*you*. I can say anything to you. You know that I'm 90% bullshit."

Riley laughed at that, loving that his comment was so close to her thoughts. "Ninety-two."

"But other girls won't know that. I can't tease them and stuff."

"You can just *tell them* you're joking."

"It's not the same," he said, shaking his head. "I do tease and joke with other women but, it's not the same. With you, I never worry about…"

Again he trailed off, and she had to hear this. "You don't worry about what with me?"

"Being a dumbass."

Okay, that surprised her. "Because I already know that you're a dumbass."

He gave her a look. "Yes," he admitted. "But you also know that I'm not a dumbass all the time."

She tipped her head. "Do I?"

He tossed his napkin at her. "Brat. You do. Because we've spent so much time together for so long that you know all the sides of me." He paused. "Well, *most* of the sides of me."

"What side don't I know?" And the answer occurred to her two seconds after she'd asked.

"The side that wants to sleep with you," he said before she could stop him.

Right. That side. The side that nearly every other woman in Sapphire Falls knew.

And it was *hugely* stupid that she felt a little jealous at that.

Because he was right. Generally, she thought of him as her brother's dumbass friend, the guy who teased her, the guy who bugged her. But yeah, she knew other sides of him too. The sweet-to-her-grandmother side. The best-friend-no-matter-what-to-her-brother side. The didn't-tease-her-but-held-her-hand-by-the-grave-and-got-her-cake side that had showed up at her grandfather's funeral.

Riley blinked hard as that memory crashed into her mind suddenly. Wow, she'd forgotten that. And the time that she'd had a fight with her mom and had driven out on a dirt road after a rainstorm and gotten her car stuck, and he was the only person she could think to call who wouldn't yell at her. He hadn't teased her that time either.

Huh.

So, okay, he might actually have some potential here. But he needed to practice.

She'd already decided that she was going to coach him, but maybe...maybe it needed to be a little more. A little more like real dating. She had to show him what having a girlfriend would really be like and make sure he was *sure* he wanted it.

"What time will you be home tonight?" she asked, getting up to refill their cups.

"Uh, not 'til late," he said. "Which is why I like to sleep in," he mentioned dryly.

Right. She'd known he'd still be in bed. That was why she'd come here. That, and the fact that she didn't really have anywhere else to go. Lucy really would be up and into her morning routine and on her way to work. Kyle and Hannah were at her mom and dad's. And Peyton would be wrapped up with Scott or busy in the bakery. Basically, everyone else she might spend time with had other stuff to do. Derek was the only one with an odd schedule like Riley's.

"I'll wait up for you."

He lifted an eyebrow. "What do you mean?"

She meant that she was going to show him that having a serious girlfriend took time and energy, even when he'd been working all night. "I'll be here when you get home and we can watch a movie or something."

"At two a.m.?" he asked.

She was a night owl, just like he was. Two a.m. didn't scare her. Her mother making waffles five hours later scared her. She nodded. "Unless you want to close up early." He'd never close up early.

"Close up the Come Again, where a bunch of people are

now coming in and working and studying?" he asked. "I don't think so."

"Okay. I'll see you after then," she said. No big deal. But she was going to have to figure out a way around her mother's morning routine.

Her eyes flickered toward the hallway that had to lead to Derek's bedroom. Hmm…

"You intend to keep me up until four a.m.?" he asked. "Especially after getting me up early this morning?"

She shrugged. "Spending time together is kind of a huge part of a relationship. You have to make it work around your schedule." That was true. And one big reason that she'd had trouble dating guys who had to be up early.

Riley made a note that he took another crepe. She actually had no idea if Lucy liked crepes, but Riley did. Not as much as waffles, but they were good. But Lucy probably did. Or she'd eat them without complaint if Riley brought them over for breakfast. Unlike Derek. She frowned. The *usual* Derek. She liked that he felt he could be himself and say what he was thinking with her.

But that was something else she had to keep in mind. She had to train Derek to go along with things once in a while even if he didn't like it. He didn't have to do that with her because she'd do what she wanted anyway. But Riley had a feeling that Derek got his way a lot with women. She'd even seen it with her own brother. Kyle liked things *his* way, for sure. But there were times when Riley had been amazed to see Derek talking her stubborn, perfectionistic brother into things.

Derek was charming and funny and had a way of saying exactly the right thing to get his way. It was good that he hadn't gone into used car sales. The entire town of Sapphire Falls would be driving old beaters around.

His charms had always been particularly effective with females. Even the girls he *didn't* date thought he was so funny and had a hard time not agreeing with him when he wanted to do things like make the prom theme vampires and werewolves —which the principal had, thankfully, shut down. Derek had done it simply to push some buttons and make people laugh. And probably to test just how much he could get away with. Which was a lot.

For every crazy, push-his-limits idea—like when he'd spread the rumor that he was going to bring strippers into the Come Again one Saturday night a month—he had four great ideas. Fundraising efforts for everything from tree planting in the park to buying an electric wheelchair for Landon Thompson. Programs like making the nursing home a daycare center during the day for little kids, mixing the children who needed supervision and activity with the older adults who needed stimulation and attention. Fun events like the town-wide snow-ball fight, and open mic night at the Come Again, where people got to sing, tell jokes, read poetry, or give motivational talks.

Derek Wright could charm anyone into doing things the way he wanted to do them, and he didn't have to worry about what the other person wanted. And that worked in these short-term hookups he had going on. But in a longer-term, more serious relationship, he'd have to be more aware of the other person. Riley was absolutely going to teach him to be aware of *her*.

They finished eating, but everything still felt awkward, between him trying to be nice and polite and her thoughts about him as a boyfriend, and a Sex God, and an honest to goodness good guy. So when he said that *since he was up so early* he was going to go check on the new sink he'd helped install at The Stop a couple days ago, Riley was relieved and said she'd clean up the kitchen.

So she did.

And then she was bored. As was her usual MO lately.

She didn't want to go home to her mom's. All of her friends

were working—or lived in another state. And even if they didn't live a couple thousand miles away, they'd be in bed. They were all night-owl computer geeks like her.

At that, she yawned. She really had gotten up early. She eyed Derek's couch. She'd bet he'd taken plenty of naps on that couch over the years. She settled onto the cushions, stretched, turned over, rubbed her cheek against the throw pillow that smelled like Derek.

And that was the last thing she remembered.

5

———————

She was asleep on his couch.

Asleep. On *his* couch. After waking him up and making him think about her nipples. And making him feel like no way could he pull off eating crepes with some nice girl he was dating and not screwing. And *then*, maybe worst of all, she'd told him that he was already doing a bunch of sweet stuff and if he kept his clothes on, he might be good at all of this.

What was *that*? Riley had complimented him? Sure, she'd seemed as surprised as he was that she thought he had a sweet side. But it was after she'd said he had potential that he'd thought he should stop teasing her and be nice.

And that had been awkward as hell.

He rolled his neck. He and Riley had a relationship. They weren't friends, exactly. They weren't related. They weren't lovers or exes. She was the only person in his life who was... what she was. Whatever it was. But he didn't want it to change. That much was clear. Having breakfast with her the way they had this morning had felt too weird.

But he wanted to have breakfast with her again. As them-

82

selves. As usual. Hell yeah, he wanted to tease her about chai seeds. What even *were* chai seeds? And crepes? Really?

He'd been thinking about that the entire time he'd checked over the pipes at The Stop, as he'd swung by to see if his grandmother's lawn needed mowed, as he'd swung by to see if Riley's grandmother's lawn needed mowed, as he'd swung by to see if Hannah's grandmother's lawn needed mowed, as he'd driven around to see if *anyone's* lawn needed mowed. But he'd just mowed for everyone so there was no lawn care to fill up his time today. Which meant that since he was up early, thanks to Riley, he had free time.

Or time to nap.

Except that his couch was full.

Normally he would take this opportunity to drop an ice cube down her back or fill her car with Styrofoam peanuts or at least change all the clocks so when she woke up, she'd think she'd slept for ten hours.

But he did none of those things. And he didn't know why. He blew out a breath and pivoted. He was going to take a shower and then...he wasn't sure.

Fifteen minutes later, he stepped out of the bathroom with a towel around his waist. Was he risking Riley being awake and still here and running into him half-naked? Yep. Why was he risking that? He wasn't any surer of the answer to that question than he had been to the one about why he didn't drop ice down her back while she was hogging his couch.

Except...maybe he wanted to see her reaction.

All of this talking and thinking about a relationship with someone he *wasn't* naked with the majority of their time together had him thinking even more about being naked and how fun that was. And thinking about how he was much better at the naked stuff. And thinking about how he was pretty good at not being naked with Riley. They drove each other crazy but it was fun. And yeah, he liked having her attention. That was definitely why he'd always done all the things he'd done. The teasing, the practical jokes, the arguing. It had been a way of having her attention when she would have just written him off as her brother's stupid friend and ignored him.

And that all got him thinking about *not* being naked with Riley.

There were lots of reasons they hadn't done that. They were like brother and sister. Kyle. Riley didn't like him. Those were just three. But he had a feeling that being naked with Riley would be like everything else was with Riley. Different from any of the other women and fun. They'd tease, they'd laugh, she'd sass him, his imagination would run. And he'd do anything to get a reaction out of her. Her reactions to him in the bedroom wouldn't be like her reaction when he'd changed all the contacts in her phone to Disney character names, but it would definitely be a reaction.

No one was better at getting a reaction out of Riley than Derek.

Unless of course she was fast asleep on his couch rather than noticing him in only a towel.

He frowned. She was getting to him, occupying his thoughts and making him analyze things he didn't want to analyze, and she was sleeping through the whole thing.

Well, no. If he was going to be up hours early and facing a day with nothing to do, she was going to be up too. Riley was no more a morning person than he was.

He pulled on some clothes and then went to the freezer. He grabbed an ice cube and headed straight for the couch.

But when he stopped next to the couch, he hesitated. The blanket that he draped over the back of his couch was now lying across her lap and upper thighs. Her feet were sticking out at the bottom and her top half was uncovered. The tank top was pulled tight over her breasts, and again Derek was distracted by the curves he'd always taken for granted before. The curves he now wanted to run his hands all over.

She looked sexy as hell. And he knew somehow it wasn't just the breasts. It was being on his couch, being completely relaxed like this, being comfortable in his space, under his blanket, her hair spread out over the pillow he used.

He thought for a second about just sliding in next to her on the couch, pulling her up against him, and napping with her. But how the fuck would he explain that when she did finally wake up?

Then he realized exactly how he would explain that. He dropped the ice cube into an empty glass sitting on the end table and then knelt on the couch cushion, easing down beside her. He shifted her gently, and she simply sighed and rolled slightly. And when he was completely stretched out, his body against hers from where her feet rested against the tops of his to where her head tucked under his chin, he put his arm around her and relaxed into the cushions.

And was able to ignore the realization that her ass settled beautifully against his cock as he drifted to sleep. Mostly.

———

Damn, it was hot in here. Why did her mom have the thermostat turned up so high?

Riley reluctantly lifted her eyelids. She was going to have to go turn on the fan or something.

But as her eyes opened, she realized it was way too light for this to be her basement bedroom. And her bedroom didn't smell like this particular scent of laundry detergent or soap or whatever she was smelling. And it definitely didn't smell like *man*.

She became aware of the weight of an arm over her and the

feel of hot hardness behind her, and she knew exactly where she was.

She was sleeping with Derek.

Riley rolled quickly. The sudden lack of heat and the thud, followed by, "Son of a bitch, Riley!" confirmed that Derek had, indeed, been napping with her on the couch.

She looked down at him with a frown. "What are you doing?"

He was rubbing his hip where it had apparently hit the coffee table. "I'm completely regretting not dropping ice down your shirt while you were sleeping."

"See, *that* I would have almost expected," she told him. "What are you doing spooning me on the couch?"

He stretched to his feet, and Riley found her eyes following his muscular form as it unfolded. "I was playing the boyfriend."

He was tall. She'd always known that. It was like the fact that water was wet. But now that she was awake and aware, her body was recalling how it felt to have all those inches pressed up against it. She tried to deepen her frown. "That's not the kind of stuff you're supposed to be practicing."

"Why not? We're not naked."

Her eyes flew to his, making her aware her gaze had been hanging out between his chest and his thighs. Part of that general area was, if she wasn't mistaken, a little more prominent than it should be.

There was something about the way he said *naked*. There was a tone in his voice or something. She felt a tingle somewhere between *her* chest and her thighs.

"The physical stuff," she said. "*That* isn't what you need to practice."

He shrugged. "I never cuddle-nap on my couch with women. So this is new. But," he gave her a little smug smile, "I think maybe I'm naturally good at this."

"This? Cuddle-napping?" she asked, using his made-up term.

"Yeah."

"What makes you think that?"

Something flickered in his eyes. "You were *very* comfortable."

She felt her eyes widen. "How do you know? I was dead asleep when you climbed onto that couch with me."

"Because of the sighing and wiggling."

Riley pushed herself up to sitting. "The what?"

"The sighing and wiggling you did against me once I was there."

Do not blush. Do not blush. He's messing with you. This is Derek. "You sure I wasn't trying to get you to move and give me more room?"

"Yeah, that doesn't explain why you brought that sweet ass right back against me when I *did* shift back a little."

She blinked at him. Her sweet ass? Had he really just said that? And insinuated that, in her sleep, she'd been trying to get as close to him as possible? Come on.

But it wasn't like being up against him had been *unpleasant*.

She pushed up from the couch, suddenly feeling antsy. He didn't step back and they were definitely sharing some personal space, but she quickly stepped around him.

"We're not doing this," she told him. "I realize that it's nearly impossible for you to shut your libido down, but this is *us*."

"We're not doing what?" he asked calmly, turning to face her as she put the coffee table between them. He set his hands on his hips, and the action drew her attention to his hips, then his abs, then everything between.

Why did she suddenly have to be aware that Derek had a body? When she'd thought of him in the past, it had been with a combination of exasperation mixed with affection. He'd just been this guy. This guy who would argue with her over the color of grass. But now he was a guy who produced exasperation and affection and confusion and...fucking tingles.

"We're not talking about asses and we're not spooning and we're not going to be thinking about each other naked."

"You were thinking about me naked?"

Maybe a little. "No. *You* were thinking about *me* naked earlier in the kitchen."

"Oh, so you *weren't* thinking about me naked? Because you sure took your time getting your eyes up to mine when I answered the door."

"You *were* half-naked. It's not like I was imagining it," she shot back, in an admittedly weak counter.

"But you didn't mind."

She blew out a breath. This was Derek. She'd called him on his shit every time she was given a chance. "You look good without a shirt on," she told him. "That's just a fact. But that doesn't mean anything. We're *us*, and I'm here to show you girl-friend stuff that's *not* naked stuff."

"We've never spooned before."

She waited for him to go on. When he didn't, she shrugged. "And?"

"So there was no way to know how good that would feel and how much you'd like it."

She sighed. She knew what he was doing. He liked to get her pissed off. So she wasn't going to get pissed off. "I guess that's true."

He looked mildly surprised that she'd agreed. "Because it *did* feel good."

Yeah, she wasn't giving him the satisfaction of getting riled up about this. Or fighting it. She lifted a shoulder. "I guess." It had. That didn't need to be a big deal. It didn't change anything.

But instead of pressing, instead of saying something like "we could do it again", instead of trying to get her to admit even more, or to blush, he just nodded and asked, "So I'll see you later at the Come Again?"

See? He teased her. But he didn't flirt with her. There was a distinct difference. It was important to remember.

Then she thought about his question. Yeah, he would. Where else would she go? She had work to do and she couldn't do it at her mom's. And there was no way she'd be going to bed before eleven. Or midnight. Or one. That was just how she was wired. Even if she was tired, she'd stay up. "I'll be there," she told him. "And then we'll come back here for movies?"

He gave her a look. "We're definitely doing that?"

"You have to put the time in," she said. "If you're going to be a bartender in a real relationship with someone who works normal hours, you'll have to figure out how to spend time together."

"But you don't work normal hours."

"But you're not actually dating me. You're practicing with me."

"But our practice sessions can happen during the day when other people are working."

"And how is that going to help you figure out how to adjust to having a real girlfriend?"

She felt a shot of warmth go through her unexpectedly. This felt good. Arguing with Derek. That was what she should be doing with him. *Not* spooning him. *Not* pressing her "sweet ass"—and she felt a little warmer when she thought about him saying that—against him.

"It's not just practicing being thoughtful and sweet and romantic? It actually matters what time of day it is?"

"This is about practical stuff like schedules and all the *other* things you can be doing with your mouth than what you're used to." She smirked. "And I feel that resisting those urges at night will be more...character building."

"You don't think I can or will go down on a woman in the middle of the day?"

Heat swept through her, and she felt her cheeks get pink. And her gaze dropped to his mouth. *Damn him*. He'd gotten to her after all. She swallowed. "I think it's harder for you to come up with *other* things to do at night. You're pretty programmed for a certain level of activity when the sun goes down."

He tipped his head. "You think you know me pretty well."

"I *do* know you pretty well."

"You don't know that side of me."

"That's because we don't spend that time of day together."

"But now we will be."

Yeah, and she was going to have to try to do it without thinking about his mouth the entire time. "Right. So I'll help you...de-program."

"You'll make me want to do *other* things with a woman alone in my house at night?"

"Right."

"No, you won't."

Why the hell was she still standing here talking about this? "We're *not* doing that stuff, Derek."

"Maybe not, but that doesn't mean you'll be able to make me want to do *other* things more. Trust me."

She blew out a breath and started for the front door. Great, now she was going to be sitting on this couch with him, watching a movie, and thinking about the things he would rather be doing. "I'll pick the movie. Just be sure you have popcorn. I like kettle corn."

Her hand was on the doorknob when he asked, "Does Lucy like kettle corn?"

Right. The woman he was practicing all of this for. And the answer to this question about Lucy, she *did* know. "Okay fine, get cheddar."

She pulled the door open and escaped before he said

anything else about Lucy. Or his mouth. Thank God. Both subjects were making Riley far jumpier than she would have liked. Or would ever admit.

———

"Hey, Riley."

Riley looked up from the website she was finishing for her brother's medical clinic to see Peyton pulling out the chair across the table.

"Hey." She grinned at the other woman. Peyton had always been a wild child. She partied hard, rebelled against most conventions, and had a mouth. Riley had always loved her. They hadn't been super close. Peyton wasn't a nerd at all. But she had a don't-fuck-with-me attitude that Riley had always admired. "How are things?"

Peyton was with Scott Hansen now. The town cop. It was the most ironic pairing ever, and Riley loved everything about it. Scott gave Peyton some very much-needed stability, and Peyton made the by-the-book guy relax a little.

"Good." Peyton grinned a grin Riley had never seen from her before. It was full of satisfaction and true happiness. "Things are really good."

"I'm glad." And she really was. Scott and Peyton were good for each other. Someday Riley would find that too. Not with a guy in Sapphire Falls. Not with a guy in *Nebraska*, God willing. But she'd eventually find someone who understood her and supported her for who she was the way Scott did for Peyton. Peyton didn't conform to many of the small-town ideals, but she could be herself with Scott. And she didn't have a mother who was always pointing out the ways that she was different, and who held to the idea that those differences were why she was unhappy.

Riley pulled her focus back to Peyton as the other woman

leaned in. Peyton had had a rough childhood, with a mom with mental illness and a neglectful father. Riley knew she should be grateful for having parents who were involved in her life and cared. But there was a tiny, selfish bit of her that kind of envied Peyton not having her parents meddling in her decisions.

"I wanted to ask you a question," Peyton said, leaning onto her forearms on the table.

"Okay, shoot."

"You can probably hack any website, right?"

Riley took her hands off her keyboard. She hadn't been expecting that question. "Um..."

Peyton grinned. "I'm not undercover for Scott or anything. I have an idea, but I wanted to run it past you before I mention it to him."

Riley ran a hand through her hair. How to answer the question? With the honest answer—which was, "yeah I can hack pretty much any website"—or the "I don't know what you've heard but it's not completely true" that she'd been giving her mother, or the safe "why do you need to know?" before spilling anything.

"Why do you need to know?" she asked.

Peyton laughed. "Okay, fair enough." But she sobered almost immediately. "I don't know how much you know about the special task force Scott is a part of, but he's been working for a few years with a group that infiltrates sex trafficking rings and works to bring them down."

Riley *hadn't* known that. "Wow. Really? Right here in Nebraska?"

Peyton nodded. "It's horrible to think about but yeah, it happens right here. He works throughout the Midwest, but there are definitely people here."

Riley frowned. "That's...awful."

"It is. And since I've been involved with him, I've been learning a lot more and getting involved too. I'm working more as an advocate. I've trained to work with girls after they get out. And I'm working to raise awareness."

Riley nodded. Now that Peyton mentioned it, she'd seen on the town's website that Peyton was raising money for a community project that would raise awareness and indicate that Sapphire Falls was a safe place for victims.

"But I was thinking about it the other night when Scott was talking about how there are websites being used to find victims. They offer things like nanny positions or other jobs, or all-expense-paid trips, or internships, and people sign up and give them all their information, agree to meet them somewhere and that's how they're taken. I was thinking that the task force could really use someone who knows all about websites and hacking to help them track the people behind them and get them taken down."

Riley shook her head. "I'm sure they have access to people who are way smarter than I am."

Peyton grinned. "I sincerely doubt it. And we're not talking about people who design sites. They need someone who knows how to get into sites and see what's behind the scenes." She leaned closer. "You hacked into a Fortune 500 company. A company with some of the highest security and tech. Right?"

It was a Fortune 100 company actually, but she didn't point that out. "I did. Accidentally."

Peyton laughed. "Accidentally? I'll give you that you didn't know what you were doing was wrong, but you did it very intentionally."

Her boss had tricked her, actually. Lied to her. Used her. Which was why the charges against her were dropped—well, that and the fact that she'd testified against him on that count as well as several others.

"Yeah, okay, I did it."

"So you could easily hack into a site these jackasses put up, right?"

"What would that accomplish?" She didn't mind the idea of hacking sex traffickers at all, of course. Those scum of the earth deserved anything and everything that happened to them. But she wasn't sure how hacking them could help.

"Is there a way to hack the site so *they* think it's still up but it's not actually visible to anyone else? They have to stay active since that's how the cops are setting up stings, but we don't want real kids finding the sites."

Riley nodded. "I'm sure I could do something. We'd have to feed it fake info but yeah, that could be done."

Peyton grinned at her. "Awesome. I figured you could. And you could probably find their bank accounts too? Phone records, travel invoices, things like that?"

"I could definitely do that."

"And you're willing to work with Scott on this?"

Do something more important than building websites for local merchants who did only about 10% of their actual business online because everyone could walk a few blocks to the actual store and get bonus town gossip while they picked up their supplies? Um, yeah.

"It would be a paid position," Peyton added.

Even better. "Have you talked to Scott about any of this?" Riley asked.

"I mentioned that I was going to talk to you about it."

Riley was surprised to feel a little streak of disappointment. This wasn't a done deal. "Oh, okay."

"But they need you," Peyton said firmly. "We have to take these people down, and the people they have working on this stuff right now just aren't good enough."

Helping to stop sex trafficking. That seemed like something even Riley's mom would approve of her doing with her "computer obsession." "Okay, talk to Scott. Let me know what he thinks."

"Great." Peyton pushed a piece of paper across the table. "And just in case you're curious."

It was a list of five websites. And of course she was curious. Did this mean that she was going to go in and start poking around even without Scott's full permission?

Oh yeah.

"Got it." She gave Peyton a smile.

Peyton pushed her chair back and stood, but hesitated.

"Something else?" Riley asked.

Peyton looked like she wanted to say more but finally shook her head. "Just check out the sites. I'll find you tomorrow and we can chat."

Riley nodded and watched Peyton head out the door. Wow, Peyton Wells leaving the bar before midnight. Things really did change.

For the next two hours, Riley scoured the websites Peyton had given her behind a privacy setting that even the Pentagon would have a hard time getting through. And by the time it was last call, Riley had made a very important decision.

She was going to help take these guys down even if Scott *didn't* give permission for her to work with the task force. They *had* to go down, and she could be a part of it. She not only had the skills, but thanks to being back in Sapphire Falls, she had the time. Not to mention the desire to prove to the world— okay, and herself—that she wasn't a complete screwup.

6

——————

"You ever sat on this couch with a girl and *not* made out with her?" Riley asked as they settled onto the two ends of Derek's sofa.

He reached for the remote and gave her a glance. "Of course."

"Who?" She picked two pieces of cheddar popcorn from the bowl she held and tossed them into her mouth.

"Peyton. Hannah. My mom." He flipped through the settings on his TV to get to the DVR.

Riley laughed. "So the answer is actually no."

"And now you," he commented as he settled back into the couch and reached for a handful of popcorn.

Okay, cheddar was good. But kettle corn was better. Riley was right on that one.

"So you've never sat on this couch with a woman you were attracted to and not made out?" Riley clarified her question.

Derek concentrated on chewing and starting the movie. Because the answer to the question was actually "not until tonight". Because, dammit, he was attracted to Riley.

Thirty-seven minutes later, she was fast asleep. And she'd

barely touched the popcorn. Cheddar was Lucy's favorite, and if he was going to have movie nights with her, that was probably a good thing to know. But now Derek wished he hadn't asked and had just gotten the kettle corn Riley had wanted. At the time, after all the talking about mouths and actually saying the words "go down on a woman" to Riley, the mention of Lucy had seemed like a good way to refocus what was going on between them. Which was nothing, really.

And if he had been picturing Riley spread out on his coffee table in nothing but a smile and her sassy attitude, well...he was only human.

He was also only human right now.

She looked gorgeous. Since they were sharing the couch, she'd fallen asleep propped up in the corner. She wore a hoodie over a tank top and loose cotton shorts that hit her mid-thigh. The hoodie was open, one breast pressing against the tank. She wasn't wearing a bra. He could tell if he looked closely. Which he wasn't. Anymore.

Her face was relaxed, and her hair was escaping from the messy bun she had on top of her head. And he could hardly count how many times in his life he'd seen her asleep. Several. Many. Yet, for some reason, tonight it hit him how damned beautiful she was. Which meant he should probably go to bed. Because he'd never had an urge to run his hand up Riley Ames's leg before, and right now he was having a hard time fighting it.

Derek got to his feet, and then leaned over to move Riley so she wouldn't wake up with a sore neck. He ignored how warm she was and how great she smelled. Mostly. Surely over the years he'd noticed that she smelled amazing. So why was it hitting him so hard tonight? And why wasn't he just waking her up to go home? But it was late. And there was no problem with her crashing on his couch. They were friends, after all.

She promptly stretched out as he pivoted her to lie down on

the cushions. Like a damned cat. With lots of arching and curling. That thrust her breasts and her sweet ass out. Yes, her ass was sweet, and yes, he'd told her so. After having it pressed up against his cock for nearly two hours while napping, he wasn't going to pretend it was anything but one of the nicest he'd had the pleasure of being pressed against. And he'd never spent two hours in that position with a woman. Taking a woman from behind simply didn't take two hours. It was one of his favorite positions, and he made sure they always thought so too. Fairly quickly.

Swallowing hard, he slid a pillow under Riley's head and then draped the blanket over her. He could send her home, but he somehow knew that she wouldn't be sleeping in at her mom's house. He was sure she'd shown up on his doorstep that morning because her mom had awakened her, either intentionally or accidentally. He'd known the Ames family long enough—hell, he'd spent the night at their house enough—to know that Riley was the only night owl in the family. The rest of them were morning people. The types who weren't just *up* at an ungodly hour, but who were happy and perky about it.

So yeah, Riley could sleep in on his couch. And then *he* could sleep in too.

He sent a quick text to her dad, letting him know she'd fallen asleep watching a movie and not to worry. Jake wouldn't check his phone until the next day over breakfast anyway, and he certainly wouldn't worry about Riley spending the night at Derek's. Honestly, if something was going to happen between him and Riley, there had been thousands of opportunities over the years. Jake trusted him.

As Derek turned off the light in the living room and headed for his bedroom, he thought about that. Not only did Erika and Jake trust him, they would probably be fine with him and Riley getting together. They loved him like a son. And they definitely found him more responsible than their daughter. They'd probably consider him a stabilizing force for Riley.

But that would be too bad.

That thought hit him as he stripped down to his boxers and slid between the sheets. Stabilizing Riley would mean changing her. And that really *would* be too bad.

That was his last thought as he drifted off.

Only to be awakened by a pounding on his door five minutes later.

When he looked at the clock, he realized it was actually three hours later. But it was pounding nonetheless. On his door. At the butt-crack of dawn. And it wasn't his front door. It was his bedroom door.

"Come on, Wright, let's go!"

He was going to kill her.

He got out of bed, stomped to the bedroom door, and yanked it open. "Jesus, Riley!"

She was standing there with a hand on her hip, clearly expecting his reaction. "I missed you." She gave him a full-of-shit grin.

"What?"

"I woke up alone." She shrugged. "And I needed to see you as soon as possible."

Okay, they were doing the this-is-what-it-would-be-like-with-a-real-girlfriend thing. Then he peered closer. "Did you go home and shower?"

She shook her head. "I went home and got my shower stuff and new clothes, but I didn't want to wake anyone up over there."

She didn't want to wake up her parents, but she had no trouble waking *him* up. And he should be annoyed by that. But he couldn't quite get past the idea that she'd been naked and wet two doors down.

He cleared his throat. "What the fuck are you doing up so early?"

"I had a nap yesterday."

Right. The nap. With him. He ran a hand through his hair. "Why do *I* have to be up right now?"

"You had a nap yesterday too."

"I didn't sleep through an entire movie last night," he told her.

"Guess you should have been more interesting to keep me awake."

He wasn't *sure* that her thoughts went where his did—namely to all the things he could have done to keep her awake—but the way she paused and her eyes widened slightly made him think maybe her thoughts did stray in that general direction. And that was...interesting.

"Lucy likes to walk."

Riley's voice was a little husky and she was looking at his mouth, so it took Derek a second to compute the four words. Then he frowned. "What?"

"Lucy likes to walk in the morning."

"I thought she likes to do yoga."

Riley nodded. Her gaze was still on his mouth, and Derek felt like she was running her fingertips over his lips. They tingled, and he wanted to *do* something with them. Something that involved the bare skin of her throat.

"She does yoga some mornings. Some mornings she goes for a walk."

And then Riley's gaze tracked lower than his mouth. And his did the same to her. She was dressed in a fitted workout tank and capri-length workout pants that hugged her—yes, sweet—ass. He bet that Lycra would be warm and silky if he ran his hand over it.

He was dressed in a lot less. He had his boxers on. Just his boxers. And he was sure that she could tell he liked the look of her in Lycra. His cock stirred even more as she made it past his chest and abs and below his waistband.

Then she licked her lips. And turned away. "I'll meet you out front."

Out front. Of his house. At just after eight in the morning. His neighbors were going to think something was wrong with him.

But, muttering under his breath about brats and early mornings, he turned back into his room and grabbed clothes and tennis shoes. He was going for a morning walk. With Riley. Because Lucy liked doing that, and if he was her boyfriend, he'd want to go with her.

As he tied his shoes, though, he admitted that no, he wouldn't *want* to go with her. But he would still do it. Because that would be a way of spending time with her that worked for their conflicting schedules and didn't involve naked time. Until afterward, when they were both sweaty.

He joined Riley on his front porch and took a moment to appreciate how she looked bent over, stretching. He didn't even think about resisting saying, "Why'd you shower *before* going for a walk?"

She looked back where she was bent over her left leg. She slowly straightened. "I didn't shower yet."

"I thought you said you showered here."

She shook her head. "I said I went home to get my shower stuff."

Oh. Why had he assumed she'd been in his shower? Because images of Riley naked and doing intimate things in his house, with him, were becoming far too regular in his mind. "So you *will be* showering here?"

She nodded. "I was actually hoping you'd let me work here today for a while."

"To avoid your mom?"

She hesitated, but eventually nodded. "Yeah. I have a new

project I want to dive into, but I don't want to tell her about it yet."

He lifted an eyebrow. "A new project?"

She chewed on the inside of her cheek but nodded.

For a second he considered teasing her about if it was legal or if it involved offshore bank accounts, but he held back. He wasn't sure why. "You're not talking about it?"

"Not to my mom."

Derek studied her face for a moment. Then he turned and started down the steps. He looked back when he realized she wasn't beside him. "You coming?"

She took a breath and then started down the steps.

They walked for about a block before he finally asked, "So, what's the project?"

He could tell she wanted to talk about it. Not with her mother, but with someone. He knew that Erika loved Riley. And worried about her. But he also knew Riley was fine. She was a little bit of a rebel, but instead of rebelling against societal norms and stereotypes or against the cliques and pressures of high school, she'd always pushed back against the expectations her parents put on her. They compared her to Kyle, Mr. Perfect, the straight-A-Mr.-Congeniality-President-of-Everything son they'd raised. And Riley had been none of those things. On purpose. It had been completely obvious to everyone, including her parents. But Erika simply couldn't help but get on Riley about the things she did or didn't do, or should or shouldn't do.

"It's for Scott."

Derek felt a surge of satisfaction in his chest when she answered. "Yeah?" He glanced at her as they turned the corner.

"It's not for sure," she said. "But Peyton mentioned it, and I figure she can talk Scott into at least considering it."

"Peyton can talk Scott into almost anything," Derek agreed with a chuckle. Scott and Peyton were perfect for each other, and he couldn't deny the tiny twinge of jealousy he felt when he saw them together. There was just something about seeing two people so in sync that made even the most cynical heart think "what if". And Derek wasn't all that cynical.

Over the next thirty minutes, they walked and Riley told him all about the project with Scott's sex trafficking task force and the websites and what she'd already learned and what she could do. They somehow ended up back at his house, and he was shocked to feel disappointed.

"It sounds amazing, Ry," he told her. "Great chance to use your super powers for good instead of evil."

For just a heartbeat she seemed annoyed. Or hurt. And he felt a stab in the general vicinity of his heart. Had he hurt her feelings? He knew that she hadn't done anything wrong out in California. He'd been kidding.

But before he could figure out what to say, she recovered and gave him a smile. "Well, the bad guys might think I'm a little evil."

Derek pulled himself together too and said, "You better make them think you're *a lot* evil."

She nodded. "Definitely."

"So, what's for breakfast today?" he asked, getting off the topic that he suddenly wasn't sure what to do with. Which he hated. It was like the awkward breakfast yesterday when he'd been trying to be sweet. But he still wanted breakfast with her today.

"Oh, I was...maybe I'll just run home after all. Mom's up by now, I'm sure." She rolled her eyes slightly, as if she couldn't help it. "And it's omelet day."

He smiled in spite of himself. At Erika Ames's house, there was definitely one day that was always omelets. As there was waffle day, cinnamon roll day, oatmeal day, muffin day, cereal and toast day—the day she needed to do something easier because she had to go to her water aerobics class—and, his favorite, bacon and eggs day.

But if Riley went home, that meant she wouldn't be showering here. Or working here. Or...here.

Fuck. Why the hell did he want her to be here?

"You need to get to work on the project," he told her. Before he could think better of it, he grabbed her hand and started up the porch steps. "You shower first. I'll make omelets here. It will be just like you're at your mom's."

Riley snorted. "I certainly hope not."

He stopped and looked back at her. "Well, you won't have anyone on your ass here."

He realized too late what he'd just said. They both seemed to freeze. Her hand was still in his, and he swore he felt the heat in his hand intensify and then spread up his arm and through the rest of his body.

Riley licked her lips. Then she pulled in a breath and said, "Yeah, that will be a nice change."

He definitely wanted to be on her ass. He wanted to be on *all* of her.

And fuck it that wasn't the most surprising and complicated and irritating thing ever. Wasn't that just typical? A *friend* was here helping him figure out how *not* to make everything about sex and what did he do? Started lusting after her, of course.

But he also wanted her to work here today. The project was good. It was a great fit for Riley. It was something that the task force needed, and it would be doing something really, really good. He didn't think Riley actually felt guilty about what had gone down in California. She'd done nothing wrong, technically. But he knew that she wanted to feel *good* about what she was doing. And right or wrong, she wanted to be able to tell her mom about her job and her passions without being judged.

He knew Riley. She could get passionate about a new level of magic in an online video game. She could get passionate about a new blog supporting women's rights and fighting for wage equality. She could get passionate about a news story, a city council issue, or a new menu item at Dottie's Diner. He'd seen all of that at different times. But he sincerely doubted that she got passionate about cyber security for banks.

"So, go shower, I'll cook, and you can work here like you'd planned," he said, letting go of her hand finally.

They needed to hang out for both their sakes. He needed to get his dick under control.

She nodded. "Okay. Thanks."

"It's not a big deal," he told her. And it shouldn't be. That was for sure.

He started the breakfast preparation. He had a hard time keeping his focus on eggs and ham and mushrooms rather than on the soapy, slick, naked woman down the hall, but he at least got points for pulling those thoughts back to whisking and flipping whenever they wandered.

And when she finally emerged, he had himself convinced that he was fine. Until he turned around. Her wet hair was up on top of her head, and she brought a vanilla-scented rush of air into the room, and she was wearing a T-shirt that said *I like you, but if zombies chase us, I'm tripping you.*

God, he liked her.

He supposed he always had, but the more time they spent one-on-one, the more apparent it became. He liked her. Not just to tease, but because she was funny and smart and mouthy and didn't think he was the best thing since fried pickles.

And her breasts looked damned good in that T-shirt. Dammit.

"Everything's ready." He gestured toward the stove.

"It smells great."

She sounded a bit surprised, but he let it go. "I'm going to shower."

"Oh, you're not—" She stopped and nodded. "Okay."

Did she want him to eat breakfast with her? Well, it didn't matter. He was going to take a shower instead of sitting here finding more things to be attracted to. Riley was gorgeous. But she wasn't for him. He was going to date *Lucy*. For one thing, Lucy didn't think he was a dumbass. Well, that might not actually be true, but she didn't have the proof of it from years of knowing him that Riley did. For another, Lucy was going to stay in Sapphire Falls forever. Just like him. Riley couldn't wait to leave. So there was that.

But when he got into the bathroom, he realized that escaping Riley and his growing attraction to her was impossible. Not just because she'd made his bathroom smell like her— a combination of vanilla and herbs and flowers that sounded in his head like it should have been nauseating, but instead had him pulling the towel she'd used to his nose and taking a deep breath. A deep, stupid, what-the-hell breath of her scent. She'd also littered the edge of his tub with shaving cream in a pink can, and a razor that was also pink, and body gel that was— God save him—pink. All of that had him thinking about the places she'd spread that shaving cream and scrubbed with that body gel.

But all of *that* wasn't the only reason he couldn't escape her. She was a part of his life. She'd been in California for the past few years, but her photos were all over Erika and Jake's house. Conversations with the Ames family usually involved Riley at some point. Most of his childhood memories—and even most after childhood—included her. And now she was living here, even if it was temporary, and their lives were so entwined that there was no way he could just avoid her or ignore her.

And he didn't want to.

He'd never been good at ignoring her. Even when she'd tried to ignore *him*, he'd had to poke at her and tease. So now that he'd realized she had the best breasts he'd ever seen in a T-shirt and that her ass really did fit perfectly against his cock, there was no way he was going to be able to keep his attention off of her.

Derek turned the shower on a little colder than usual and shed his clothes. And stopped trying to pretend that he didn't want Riley. What would she be like in bed? Sassy, he was sure. Probably up for anything. That was how she did everything else, why would sex be any different?

He braced a hand on the wall, letting the shower spray rain down on his head. He closed his eyes and did the inevitable. He took his cock—his hard-for-Riley cock—in hand and started stroking.

He could easily imagine her on her knees in front of him. Not submissive—though getting bossy with her would be a hell of a lot of fun—but because she'd want to drive him crazy. She'd watch his every reaction to what she did to see how best to push him, to make him curse under his breath, to make him lock his knees so he didn't go down and grasp for something to hold him up. She'd lick and suck and stroke until he was saying her name and gripping her hair, his need and ultimate surrender obvious. And then, before he could get to the sweet release, she'd stand up and tell him bluntly, "Fuck me, Derek". She'd demand that he give as good as he got. So he'd lift her up against the wall and pound into her. She'd take every inch, every thrust. She'd dig her fingers into his back and would urge him on with "more" and "yes" and "harder".

Derek squeezed his cock and stroked harder, sliding up and down his shaft, eyes shut, a clear vision of Riley in his head. He could easily imagine the hot, slick hold on his cock was her pussy. He could hear her voice in his head telling him exactly what to do to make her come, and he'd gladly do it. He wouldn't kid around or tease or joke. He'd fuck her to the point that she had to admit he was a damned Sex God after all.

He felt his orgasm coming on fast and hard. His gut clenched, his balls tightened, and he erupted. He kept from shouting or groaning, knowing she'd hear from the kitchen, but barely. In fact, part of him wanted her to hear it. Wanted her to know that she was getting to him, and while she might consider it a small victory to be driving him nuts, he wasn't going to let her get away with it for long. If he was going to be crazy, so was she.

As he finished showering, dried, and dressed, he marveled at how he should be feeling relieved and relaxed after a hard, satisfying orgasm, but how, instead, he felt even more irritated than before. Maybe Riley didn't know she was getting to him, but *he* knew it. And hell, she wasn't even trying. That was maybe the worst part. If she'd been trying to tease or seduce him, that might be one thing. It could have turned into a fun game of chicken—see who could make the other one beg first. But no, she was just being Riley.

And a big part of him couldn't help but think that if he hadn't been sexually attracted to her before he'd spent a few innocent hours alone with her, then he really was a dumbass.

By the time he made it back to the kitchen, Riley was done eating and had cleaned up everything except for a plate and a set of utensils. She flipped an omelet from the pan she held onto the plate and handed it to him. He'd made her an omelet and she'd made him one. That shouldn't feel significant. And maybe it wasn't. But the fact that she hadn't added asparagus or avocado or some weird nuts or seeds, and the fact that he didn't comment on that, or tease her about what gross things he might have secretly added to hers, was significant. Things were changing between them. They were hanging out, talking, and he was thinking about her breasts far too much.

She washed the pan as he ate. Then she grabbed a bag from the living room and started setting up her computer, mouse pad, and wireless keyboard on the table across from him.

"This still okay?" she asked, as she plugged into the outlet behind her.

"Of course."

"What are you doing today?"

He hadn't really thought about it. He was going to do some painting in the new addition at the Come Again at some point, and he needed to get the scaffolding out and clean the light fixtures in the vaulted ceiling at the Methodist church. He shrugged. "Just some stuff."

"You're working tonight?"

"Yep." He worked almost every night.

"'Til close?"

He frowned. *This* was the part of the dating thing that he didn't like. He didn't really make a lot of plans ahead of time, and he hung out with people who didn't either. His two best friends were more or less on call twenty-four seven around here, and neither really knew what might come up at any minute. Those relationships worked for Derek. He just went with the flow. "Yeah, 'til close. Not sure what time I'll get there. Bryan's covering until I show up."

Riley looked up and gave him a little frown. She must have heard the annoyance in his tone. "You know, when you're dating someone, it's okay for them to know where you are and when."

"Every second?"

"Of course not. But it's not unreasonable to ask what time you get off work."

He shoved back from the table and took his dishes to the sink. "Yeah, well, *we're* not actually dating."

If they were, the scenario in his head during his shower would *not* have been fictional. He scowled as he rinsed his plate. He didn't want to date Riley, dammit. They'd be a terrible match. They'd kill each other.

"So?" she asked. "I thought you wanted a taste of what this would really be like."

He swung around. "You're offering me a *taste*?" he repeated. "Well, Ry, I'm all over that. I know exactly where I'd start, in fact. But if you want me checking in with you on where I am and what I'm doing every damned second, you can forget it."

She looked exasperated. "What's your problem?"

"Jacking off in the shower while thinking of a girl who's basically been my kid sister all my life."

Her mouth dropped open. She shook her head. "You're just saying that to shock me or whatever."

He wished like hell that was true. He pushed away from the counter. "I'm leaving."

"Fine. I'll probably just be here for a few hours and—"

"Whatever. You don't have to report in to me either." He stomped through the house, grabbing a pair of jeans off the back of one of the chairs and his work boots by the door. It was too hot to wear them at the church, but he never knew when he might get a call to climb up into someone's hay loft or something else that would require different attire.

See? He didn't have to *plan* every damned thing out. He was just always prepared for anything.

Except for Riley.

He definitely hadn't been prepared to have her around more, in his house, in his business, in his *head*.

He stopped at the front door and started to turn back. But he didn't want to ask the question in his head just then. He gripped the doorknob. *Don't do it. Don't fucking do it.*

And he didn't.

Until he got to his truck. Then he texted her. *Will you be in tonight?*

He knew she'd know he meant at the Come Again. That was one thing about "dating" Riley. He saw her every night at the bar. They kept the same hours. When she wasn't dragging his ass out of bed at the crack of dawn.

That meant that if they really *were* dating, they'd have plenty of time to go on walks and have meals together and... shower together.

He swore and tossed his phone on the seat next to him, starting the truck and pulling out of his drive.

But a minute later, when his phone dinged with a text, he reached for it. He pulled up at the stop sign at the end of the block and opened the message. It was from Riley.

Yes.

That was all. But he was relieved.

I want you to taste test a couple new pizzas, he sent back. The pizza business was going to be all his, and he was excited. It was still a couple months away from opening, but at the same time, he felt like he was running out of time to get things done. And he was getting nervous. He never got nervous. He never had a reason. But he supposed that was a sign that this business really mattered to him.

He realized he was holding his breath, waiting for Riley's response. The truth was, he wanted to see her tonight. He didn't want to have to give her a minute-by-minute account of his day, and he didn't need that from her either. But he was curious about what she'd be up to, and he knew by eight, when she usually came in, that he'd wonder where she was if she didn't show. And that was so fucking stupid.

Great. I love pizza was her return message.

He tossed the phone onto the seat again, realizing that he was far too pleased by her answer.

But Riley would tell him the truth about the pizza. That he could be sure of. If they sucked, she'd have no trouble breaking the news. These were not the typical pepperoni or everything pizzas that most people were used to. He'd have those too, but his were going to be stone-oven pizzas, so a little different from the pizzas people ate around here now, and he wanted to have a couple specialties. Barbecue chicken was one. Philly cheesesteak was another. The ones he'd sampled in Omaha had been good, but he hadn't tried to reproduce them. For some reason, tonight seemed like a good time. Maybe it was because Riley told him about the task force project. Maybe that had opened up a new state where they actually told each other things and had serious discussions instead of him just constantly trying to push her buttons. Huh. Maybe they *were* going to be able to be grown-ups together.

At least if he quit saying things like, "I jerked off in the shower thinking of you."

He'd hoped that if she knew he wanted her opinion on something, she'd definitely come in tonight. He'd been 90% sure she would anyway, but that was before he told her about the shower. No doubt that could make things awkward. So he wanted to be sure she came into the bar. And Riley loved to give him her opinion.

But, for a change, he *wanted* her opinion.

It's just pizza, he told himself as he turned into the church parking lot.

But his new business wasn't just pizza. It was a chance to do something totally on his own, a chance to bring something new to the town, a chance to be an actual business owner instead of working for someone else all the time.

And it was a chance to spectacularly fail. He didn't have those chances very often. The things he did were pretty safe in general. So this was new.

He supposed that was also why it felt like bringing Riley in on things fit. Their relationship had always been safe. They were just...there. In each other's lives. He showed up, he teased her, she got annoyed, she left. Then the next time, it started all over again. He knew which buttons to push, knew which reactions he was going to get. Now though...things between them didn't feel as predictable. Or safe.

So maybe he was just in the risk-taking mood.

Of course, it was equally likely that he was doing something really stupid here.

7

———

She'd spilled her guts to Derek. And he'd jerked off in the shower thinking of her.

Things were so not normal between them that she honestly didn't know what to do.

Riley was still sitting at Derek's kitchen table, her laptop open, staring at a blank screen twenty minutes after he'd left.

What the *hell* was happening?

She'd told him all about the task force project, and she knew she'd been letting her enthusiasm show. Last night with Peyton it had all been new, but now that she'd had a chance to think it through and do some research, she was feeling excited. She'd even confessed to feeling flattered. Typically, that would be the perfect fodder for Derek to tease her.

But he hadn't. He'd listened. He'd asked questions. He'd said he thought she'd be great at it.

And then he'd apparently jerked off in the shower thinking about her.

Riley felt her cheeks—and a few other places—get hot. *Surely* he'd been kidding about that. But why? She'd been asking him about his plans for the day and wondering when she might see him. And then he'd said *that*. And he definitely hadn't seemed like he was teasing.

God.

She put her hands to her cheeks. She could not get that out of her head. She'd seen enough of Derek's body to fill in the blanks for what she hadn't. And the images of him in the shower, water cascading over his back and chest and abs, his hand wrapped around his cock, stroking himself and thinking of her...Riley squeezed her thighs together and took a shaky breath. She could not sit here, at his kitchen table, and think all of the things she was thinking. Most especially the thought where she offered to help next time.

That was just not what she and Derek were. She was, as he'd said, like a little sister to him. And he was a pain in her ass. And what they'd always had was...nice.

That thought surprised her but as she thought about it, she had to admit that, yeah, it *had* been nice. It hadn't always felt that way. In fact, until that very moment, she'd definitely not thought of it as nice. But Derek was predictable. She always knew how he would react to things. Sure, it was with teasing and banter. Yes, it seemed that he had a hard time taking anything seriously. Absolutely it seemed that she couldn't say anything without him adding his two stupid cents.

But at the same time, it had always been generally good-natured. She knew what it was like to be criticized for real. Her mother did it on a regular basis. So she definitely could tell the difference between that and what Derek did. Derek teased. He tried to make her smile. He didn't let her take things— including herself— too seriously.

Riley sat up straighter in her chair as she thought back over their interactions and the general vibe between her and Derek over the years.

Yes, that was it. He'd teased her. He'd always been there, seemingly in the way. Seemingly always with something to say, some comment to make. But it had always been lighthearted. And it had very often been in front of her mother. As if reminding her not to get too worked up about things. As if to help her see the situation less seriously.

Had he done that intentionally? Or was that just who he was?

Derek was different from Kyle. Kyle did worry about things like schedules and doing things a certain way, getting things right. Her mother and father were the same. Riley was the one person in her family who didn't do everything according to the "rules" and, now that she thought about that, Derek was more like her than any of *them*. He wasn't really a rebel. He took care of the entire town. And yet, he kept strange hours and just rolled with the punches and did things his way. Because he was always doing things for other people, no one got too worked up about him being exactly on time or how he got things done, but yeah, he'd managed to work it out so that he pretty much did whatever he wanted, when he wanted to do it.

That was really her style as well. She loved working in cyber security because she could set her own hours, work mostly remotely, and did things her way because most people didn't really understand what she did in the first place.

Derek would get that.

Her mother and brother, not as much.

How had she never realized all of this about Derek before? That they had several key things in common? That his teasing had annoyed her, but it had never felt like criticism? And that even when it annoyed her, it didn't *really*. She knew that he was just working to get a rise out of her, and she gave in to that. For some reason.

And now he wanted her to taste test his pizzas. He wanted her opinion on something.

And then there was that jerking-off thing…

Mentally shaking herself, she put her hands back on her

keyboard. She was going to *work* now. All of this was a lot of realization for one day. And she didn't like the way desire pulsed through her anytime she thought of him just down the hall, his hand on his—

Somehow she managed to work for about ten minutes. But it turned out to be nearly impossible for her to keep her mind on anything *but* Derek. Of course, sitting in the middle of his kitchen probably had something to do with that. She needed a change of scenery.

But there simply weren't many options for that in Sapphire Falls. The only place to really work quietly without interruption was the Come Again after hours. If she went home, her mom would pull her into a project, or would want to chat about how long Riley thought Kyle and Hannah would wait before they got married. Everywhere else in town would be overrun with people she'd known her whole life who would want to sit and chat and ask a million questions. Which was exactly why she'd started going to the Come Again in the first place.

She sat back in her chair and yawned.

This getting up early to get *Derek* up early was starting to wear on her. She could see his couch from where she sat, and she had to admit that it was one of the more comfortable couches she'd ever lain on.

Derek would be out for a while.

She was going to be up late tonight. And she'd kind of enjoyed their morning walk, so she might have to get him up early again tomorrow.

Yeah, she needed a nap.

She closed up her computer and tucked everything back into her bag. Then she pulled her bun down and shook her hair out. She yawned widely as she lay down where she'd spent the night, snuggling into the pillow that smelled like Derek.

———

She was asleep on his couch again.

Derek stood at the end of the couch, watching Riley for a long moment. She slept like the dead. He hadn't been quiet when he'd come into the house. In fact, he'd made more noise than he'd really needed to. Her car was still in his drive and he'd assumed she was working. And yeah, he'd wanted to distract her. Just like when they were kids and he'd make up excuses to go into the kitchen where she was studying, or through the living room when she was trying to watch TV. He wanted her attention.

But even stomping his feet on the porch and letting the front screen door slap shut hadn't awakened her.

He shook his head. Poor thing. She was exhausted from keeping him up late and getting him up early. He started to reach out to tickle her foot, but he paused just before touching her.

His eyes slowly climbed up the length of her leg to the curve of her ass, then up to the strip of skin peeking out where her shirt had ridden up on her waist. And suddenly he had a better idea. Or a more fun idea, anyway.

He'd been thinking about her all day. About how she'd driven him to get himself off in the shower. About how he'd announced that fact to her. About her stunned reaction.

And now she was asleep on the couch. As if she had nothing on her mind at all. Certainly nothing that would cause her to toss and turn instead of sleep.

Yeah, he simply wasn't wired to let Riley be. Especially when *he* was worked up over *her*.

He pivoted and headed for the bathroom, stripping as he went, dropping his clothes on the floor wherever they came off. This was how he lived when he didn't have a guest. And it was how he'd live if he had a serious girlfriend.

Might as well practice.

In the bathroom, he cranked up the radio that sat on one end of the vanity. He banged cupboards open and shut. He padded through the living room to the kitchen, naked, to retrieve his electric screwdriver from the cupboard by his back door. Then he'd headed back into the bathroom to tighten the screw on the towel rod. Yeah, he could have used a regular screwdriver, but the electric screwdriver was faster and would get the screw nice and tight. And it was a lot louder.

He returned the screwdriver to the cupboard, walking back through the living room as if he owned the joint. Which he did.

A glance at the couch showed that Riley was sleeping through it all.

Or at least she had her eyes shut.

He didn't stop and study her, but he did see that her breathing wasn't quite as soft and even as before, and he had a suspicion that she was sneaking a peek.

Exactly as he'd planned.

He grinned and headed back into the bathroom. He showered for the second time, rinsing off the dirt he'd cleaned out of the arched ceiling at the church and the dirt and grease he'd acquired from changing Gladys Jenkins's tire when he'd seen her pulled over on his way between the church and the community center, where he'd pulled a bunch of chairs out of the storage area in the basement.

And as he showered, he used his hand on his cock only to apply soap. But he definitely thought of Riley and knew that she was now lying on his couch, thinking about him in the shower, and what he'd told her about his *earlier* shower.

He was whistling along to Brett Young by the time he shut the water off and started toweling off.

But he left the towel in the bathroom.

He walked down the hall to his bedroom, the way he always did. Which took him right past the doorway that opened into the living room.

He didn't look in, but he heard her.

And what he heard froze him in mid-step.

It was a moan.

And then, "Derek," said in a husky, needy voice.

He slowly turned. Riley was still on the couch, her eyes were still shut—but her hand was down the front of her shorts.

Derek's mouth went dry and his cock swelled. He braced his hands on either side of the doorway, his eyes locked on her. She arched her back, wiggled her hips, and did the "Derek" thing again. Then she opened one eye.

Busted. She was faking. Trying to drive him nuts.

Of course she was.

"Well, don't stop now, Ry," he said, his voice a little gruffer than he'd intended. "Do what you need to do."

She jerked her hand from her shorts and let out a short, irritated breath. She swung her legs over the side of the couch and frowned at him. "Really? You're just going to stand there, buck naked, and watch as if this isn't the weirdest situation we've ever been in?"

He felt his skin begin to burn as her gaze tracked over his body. He had no hang-ups about being naked. He did a lot of manual labor. Staying toned and fit was one perk of that. He lifted his hands and curled his fingers into the top of the door-jamb, leaning in slightly and giving her an unobstructed view of, well, everything.

"*That*," he said, nodding toward her and the couch, "would be well worth a few minutes of awkwardness afterward when I remembered who you are."

"You would forget?" she asked, her eyebrows climbing toward her hair.

"I might get distracted." He let his eyes wander over her, from the top of her head to her toes. He couldn't see everything in between clearly, with her sitting hunched over, but he didn't need to see it to want it.

He wondered if Riley realized that, at this moment, everything was changing.

He wanted her. He wasn't sure when it had happened *exactly*. It felt like he should be able to pinpoint a moment. Like when she'd brushed against him at his front door a few days ago. Or sometime when she walked into the Come Again looking hot and sassy and he'd felt a physical reaction. But honestly, it felt like it had come on a lot slower than that. Like it had been happening bit by bit for a long time. A very long time. Like maybe forever.

Derek felt his body harden and heat even more with that thought. He was shocked. He would have expected mixing more emotion and history into everything would cool some of his desire. But it was definitely not working that way.

"I swear, if you call me some other girl's name, I'll cut that thing off," Riley said, coming to her feet.

"This thing?" He couldn't help but grin at that. "You'll need a lot of upper body strength to get through something this size."

She snorted. "God, you're such an ass."

"Because I'm driving you crazy with lust?"

She took a deep breath and, much to his surprise, nodded. "Yeah."

"You could leave." But he'd go after her if she did. That was just as surprising as the rest of what he was feeling.

She nodded again, slower. "Yeah, I could." She licked her lips. "But I'm not going to."

"Thank God," he said, sincerely.

She crossed the room, coming to stand right in front of him. He kept his hands up on the doorframe, but everything in him strained to reach for her. She met his eyes.

"Did you really do what you said?"

"The shower thing?"

"Yes."

He thought about his answer. And the fact he was completely naked. And she was standing not six inches away from him. "Before I answer, you need to really think about whether you *want* the answer," he told her. "And what you're going to do with it once you know."

She pulled her lower lip between her teeth and shocked him by looking vulnerable for a second. "If you were kidding and said that just to mess with me all day, I don't know if I can be responsible for what I do."

Holy crap, she was afraid he'd been teasing her. And yet she was still standing here, in front of him, asking for the truth. And admitting that she was going to be upset if he'd lied.

He *had* been an ass to her in the past. For sure. When he wasn't sure that she wanted him around. When he wasn't sure she was paying attention. Now he knew. She *did* want him. She was absolutely paying attention.

Derek dropped his arms and reached for her in one motion. He cupped her face, pulling her forward. He looked into her eyes in a way he never had before. Intently. Ready to be fully honest. And vulnerable himself. Because she could hear his answer and then laugh and say *she* was the one who was kidding around.

"I absolutely got myself off thinking about you and your sassy mouth and your sweet ass and...everything else about you," he said, honestly. Yeah, it had been mostly a physical fantasy in the shower, but he knew deep down that there was no way this could ever be just physical with him and Riley. "And," he continued when he realized she was holding her breath, "I would really like to do it all for real."

She sucked in a quick breath, her pupils dilated, and she licked her lips again.

Derek wasn't sure he'd ever been as turned on in his life. This was crazy. He was used to foreplay, or at least a few hours of flirting at the bar, before getting naked with someone. He and Riley had done none of that.

Or had they had *years* of foreplay? It had never felt that way before, but now that the whole how-long-have-I-had-feelings-for-Riley question had occurred to him, he couldn't shake the idea that maybe they'd been headed in this direction for a long time.

"If we do this, things will be...complicated."

He thought about that. "I don't know, Ry. This feels really fucking easy."

"I'm sure girls are always easy for you when you're brandishing *that*." She gestured in the general vicinity of his cock.

And he laughed. "Thanks. But that's not what I meant." He took a breath, and sobered slightly. "Being with *you* is easy. Telling you that I've been thinking about your nipples for three days straight is easy. And telling you that I really like you, and that you make me laugh, and that I think you being a computer hacker for the cops is kick-ass, and admitting that I really want you to like my pizza or it's going to make me doubt everything, is easy. And none of that is easy with anyone else."

She was staring at him, and Derek absorbed the moment he'd struck Riley Ames speechless.

But a second later she said, "Well, holy shit, Derek."

He nodded. That summed this all up pretty perfectly. "Yeah."

She took a breath. "You know what else I think is going to be easy?"

"What?"

"Having multiple orgasms with you."

He gave a short laugh, again surprised.

"So show me this Sex God stuff, already."

That's all he needed to hear. He lowered his head and kissed her.

———

Derek Wright was kissing her.

And he was naked.

And he wanted to have sex with her.

Riley's head was spinning as Derek took her mouth. And he *took* her mouth. He didn't go in soft and gentle. With his hands on her face, he pulled her up onto her tiptoes, covered her mouth, and stroked his tongue boldly along her lower lip, demanding entrance.

She gripped his biceps and gladly gave him that entrance. Her whole body was instantly hot and tingly, and she met his strokes with her tongue, suddenly hungry. She arched closer and remembered, happily, that he was already naked. Completely. Gloriously. She had been standing there, talking to him, half teasing and half feeling more vulnerable than she could remember feeling with a guy since maybe high school, and he'd been naked the whole time.

And the guy looked *good* naked.

But even with six-pack abs and what had to be a good nine inches of Sex God equipment hadn't kept them from their usual joking. Which felt nice. Right. Comfortable.

And like she had never wanted anyone the way she wanted Derek.

It was as if once she let the thoughts into her head, she couldn't stop the heat and need from taking over. As soon as she got over how weird it was to kiss him, she was going to enjoy the hell out of this.

And she got over it in about five seconds.

The guy was, at the very least, a Kissing God.

Riley ran her hands up Derek's arms to his shoulders, then down over his chest. Oh yeah, all the hauling stuff all over town for everyone was a very good thing. For them, of course, but definitely for her right now.

Derek's hands dropped from her face to her ass, pulling her more firmly up against him. She ran her hands down his rib cage and gripped his waist, also helping get her body closer to his. But there wasn't quite enough leverage. Or he was too tall. Or something.

She started to pull back to mention all of this, but suddenly Derek turned her, put her up against the wall next to the doorway, and pressed close.

And yeah, that totally worked. Now he was able to press close everywhere. *Everywhere.* He felt amazing. Hot, hard, and eager. His hands roamed, his mouth was hungry, and Riley felt a dizzying rush at how much he seemed to want her.

She let her hands roam as well. Down to the magnificent ass, then around to the cock she'd been thinking about all day. When she stroked him, Derek jerked his head back, his breath hissing out.

"Ry," he groaned.

She stroked up and down his length, and he leaned in to put his forehead against hers.

"Did you imagine it like this in the shower?" she asked.

He reached up and circled his hand around hers, squeezing tighter around his cock. "No."

She let him move her hand up and down, the hard heat of him making her deep muscles clench and her body feel like it was melting. "No?"

"It was your mouth." His voice was gruff.

And Riley felt a shaft of heat shoot through her. "My mouth, huh?"

He gripped his cock, his hand still around hers. "Yeah. Your sweet, sassy mouth, taking me in, sucking me."

She took a shaky breath. "Oh."

He gave a soft chuckle. "It was pretty hot."

"I can do that."

He let out a breath. "I bet you can."

Suddenly, she wanted to do it. She started to dip her knees, but he wouldn't let her go.

"But you know...I have a better idea."

"A better idea than a blowjob?" she asked. "Is there such a thing?"

"How about you tell me?"

Then he dipped *his* knees, sinking to the floor in front of her.

Riley caught her breath. "I don't know, Sex God. Not sure you're the one that's supposed to be kneeling."

"Give me five minutes and *then* let me know how you feel about that."

His fingers went to the waistband of the yoga pants she wore, and he skimmed them and her panties off in one smooth move.

He gave a little growl of appreciation, his eyes hot on the area between her legs as she lifted one foot at a time to kick the clothes out of the way.

"Just as I imagined," he said, his voice rough. Then he gripped her butt in both hands and leaned in, kissing the area just inside her hip bone.

She was completely unable to pursue the whole topic of him imagining this because his hot mouth on her bare skin swamped her system with sensations. All she could do was grip the top of his head with one hand and flatten the other on the wall behind her to keep herself upright.

Her head fell back, thunking against the wall, her eyes sliding shut as heat and want washed over her.

Derek swirled his tongue around the belly button ring she wore, then kissed across her stomach over the swirling design of the cherry blossoms tattoo that ran hip to hip. He paused every couple of centimeters to give a flower a little flick of his tongue.

"*Derek*," she gasped as he drew closer to where she was unbelievably wet and hot. Sure, having a good-looking, naked guy kissing her *should* make her wet. But this was Derek, and she was realizing as good as he was with his mouth in *this* situation, she really kind of loved his mouth all around. Yes, even when he was teasing. Certainly when he was charming her grandmother. Absolutely when he was saying things like "I'll get it taken care of" to someone who needed his help. And when he made her brother or mom laugh and relax. And when he smiled. And when he—

He dipped his head and licked over her clit, and Riley's thoughts all went to *this. This* was all she cared about at this moment. Her fingers curled into his hair, and she gasped and arched closer to his tongue without even thinking. She was just feeling, and what she felt was that she wanted *more*.

"Lift up. Let me get a good taste," he said huskily, his hand going to her knee and lifting.

Mindlessly, she let him lift her leg and prop her knee over his shoulder. It opened her up, and she had no time to even think about thinking about being self-conscious. Derek dove in like a starving man on chocolate cake. He licked again, his tongue dipping lower this time, then returned to suck on her clit before saying hotly, "You taste fucking amazing, Riley."

She sagged against the wall, grateful he was holding her as if he was never going to let her go. Sure, his tongue was magic and he knew exactly how to use it. Sure, she was hot and ready for him. But there was something about him talking to her, and using her name, so there was absolutely no way for either of them to forget who they were doing this with, that made her boneless in a very delicious and unexpected way.

"Derek," she said again, breathless, but wanting his name in the air too.

"Take your shirt off, Ry," he said, lifting his head and looking up at her.

The heat in his eyes made her reach for the bottom of her

tee without any further prompting. He watched her strip it off and reach behind for her bra clasps. Her nipples were so hard they nearly ached as she tossed her bra away.

"The *exact* shade of pink I pictured," he told her.

She couldn't stand it. She cupped her breasts, squeezing slightly, trying to relieve the tingling.

He groaned and ran his hand up her back, urging her forward so he could take one in his mouth. The heat and suction made her inner muscles clench hard, and she suddenly felt achy and empty.

"Derek." She sounded like she was begging for something. And she was, essentially. She was begging for *him*.

"I've got you, Ry," he promised darkly. Then he lowered his head between her legs again.

She pushed back against the wall, needing to feel something solid, and closed her eyes again as pleasure poured through her.

His tongue worked on her clit and he slid two fingers into her, giving her some of the pressure she needed. She pressed closer, he sucked and thrust harder, and suddenly she felt the orgasm coming on, fast and sharp.

"Come on, Ry. Give it to me."

She cried out as the sensations hit, igniting all of her nerve endings.

"That's my girl." Derek kept stroking her with his fingers, slower now, as she came down from the heights.

There was something in his tone that made her open her eyes and look down. He was now watching her face...and there was an affection in his expression that suddenly made her feel tears sting her eyes. She blinked rapidly and made herself smile. "So far, so good, Sex God."

He grinned and stretched to his feet. Slowly. Rubbing his body along hers as he straightened. Then he cupped her face again and kissed her. It was deep and hot like before, but he moved slower this time, as if drinking her in.

"Bedroom," he said simply, lifting his head after what felt like an hour.

Her body was still humming with the aftereffects of her orgasm, and she wasn't sure she could make her legs go even the ten feet it would take to get to his bedroom. "Here," she told him.

"Condoms are in the bedroom."

"I'm on the pill right here."

He paused and stared down at her. "You're okay without a condom?"

"Do I have a reason to worry?"

He shook his head. "I'm clean."

She knew he got around, but she also believed he was responsible about it, and she trusted him if he said he was good to go. "Me too."

Without another word, he put his big hands on her ass and lifted her. She wrapped her arms and legs around him, feeling his cock nudging at her entrance.

"You ready?" He gave her a grin that would have gotten her ready if she wasn't, just by itself.

She nodded. "So, so ready."

And he moved his hips, sinking deep, nice and slow. She felt her breath catch in her chest, and her toes actually curled. When he was as deep as he could get and she felt every glorious inch, he paused. His jaw was tight as he asked, "You okay?"

She realized she'd been holding her breath as she laughed. "Yeah, Big Guy, I'm okay. You're very impressive, but I can handle it."

His eyes flashed and the corner of his mouth curled. "You think so?"

A surge of what she could only label as happiness went

through her. Okay, they were having sex. But this was still Derek. This wasn't going to change anything. "I'd love for you to try to get me to the point where I *can't*," she told him.

His grin grew, but his eyes darkened. "Well, what kind of god would I be if I didn't perform some miracles?"

Riley squeezed her muscles around him and curled her fingers into his shoulders. "Miracles huh?"

"Yeah, like making Riley Ames say, 'I was wrong and you were right, Derek.'"

She laughed. "That *would* be a miracle."

"Well, hang on, sweetheart. Here we go." He gripped her ass and pulled out, slowly, the friction so, so good.

Then he thrust, deep and hard. Riley felt it *everywhere*. The bottoms of her feet even tingled, and she let out a heartfelt moan.

And then he picked up the pace. He thrust and withdrew in deep, steady strokes that were fast and hard and hit absolutely every single spot that she needed him and a few she hadn't ever felt before. She hung on, for sure. She really felt like she was doing very little to help the whole scenario out. But she couldn't feel bad about it. She just wanted to *feel*. She just wanted...Derek. All of him. His body, his humor, their history, and, for sure, that half-hot, half-affectionate look he'd been giving her.

She felt the orgasm building from down deep, a sensation she could never reproduce herself. She tightened her arms and legs around him, feeling the crest coming closer quickly.

"Oh, not quite yet, darlin'." Suddenly Derek pulled back.

"Wha— *What*?" she demanded as the delicious pace went from perfect to nothing.

He let her go, her feet swinging to the floor.

"Der—"

But before she could even get his name out, he spun her to face the wall. "Hands up, sweetheart."

She'd barely braced her hands on the wall before he gripped her hips and thrust, filling her again from behind and hitting a spot that made her cry out.

"That's right. That's fucking *right*," he said gruffly. "Let me hear it."

Nothing had ever felt like this. Ever.

And this was *Derek*.

And that somehow made it even better.

His thrusts were deep and sure, and the way he held her hips kept her exactly where he wanted her. Exactly where she wanted to be.

He said dirty things, he touched her all over—like a freakin' Sex God— and she was quickly climbing toward another orgasm.

She'd *known* those would be easy with him.

"Come for me. God, I need to feel it, Ry."

Well, if he insisted. She reached back and gripped his ass, holding him tight as she went over the edge, calling his name.

He was right there with her. "Fuck, Ry. Yes! Fuck."

She knew she might have bruises on her hips where he was hanging on. And she hoped she would. Because she wasn't going to believe this happened when it was over.

Derek kept moving even as the ripples of pleasure faded. Finally, he braced his hand on the wall over her head, leaning into her, putting his mouth against her ear.

"Riley."

That was all he said.

That was all he needed to say.

She covered his hand on her hip and squeezed. "Derek."

8

———

So Riley Ames had just rocked his world.

He'd expected it to be good. To be really good.

He hadn't expected to want to throw her over his shoulder, carry her to bed and never let her leave. He was always pretty ready for them to leave. He never wanted to *keep* them. He had to-go coffee cups, for fuck's sake.

But he never wanted Riley to drink coffee anywhere else.

Damn, this *had* gotten complicated and messy. Really fucking fast.

He finally kissed her shoulder and moved back. She turned in his arms, and they kissed long and deep. He couldn't keep his hands off her ass.

"Let's go to bed," he said against her lips, squeezing that ass.

But he felt her push him back. She pressed her lips together and looked up at him, adorably disheveled and flushed.

"We probably shouldn't do that."

He lifted a brow. Oh, they definitely should. "Why not?"

He could tell she was considering not telling him what she was really thinking. He squeezed her ass. "Don't lie to me, Ry."

If she was surprised he knew what she was thinking, she

131

didn't show it. She took a breath. "Because if we go to bed, we're both not getting anything else done today and you'll be late to work."

Okay, that was all true. And hearing her say it was hotter than hell. He leaned in and kissed her, then said, "Sounds about right."

"And we can't do that."

"Why not?"

"The guy who's always around, doing everything for everyone, suddenly disappears for a day? I think they'll notice."

"They?" But yeah, they would.

"The whole entire town." She pushed him back, and his hands slipped from her butt.

He sighed.

She laughed. "Yeah, being the town's favorite person might have a drawback or two."

Normally having stuff to do, places to go, people waiting for him to show up, was a fantastic excuse to get gone. Now, he was regretting everything.

And that was, actually, what pulled him out of the Riley daze. He didn't want to have to report in about everything he was doing to anyone, and he didn't want someone coming along and changing up his routines and, hell, his life. He liked things the way they were. Being with a woman who he'd grown addicted to within only a few days of hanging out and after fucking her once against the wall was *not* a part of the plan here.

That hit him right in the chest. He was looking for a relationship, but he was looking for one with someone who wouldn't mess with his life and who wouldn't—and he cringed even thinking it—be someone he could be so wrapped up in, he wouldn't want to do anything else.

Shit.

Fuck.

Damn.

That was a crappy way to approach a relationship. Even he knew that. If he didn't want to be involved in someone else's life and have them involved in his, then he shouldn't be *in* a relationship.

Which was exactly why he'd avoided it until now.

His dad tried to juggle everything—his interests and the things he needed and wanted to do, with his wife's constant need for reassurance—and it never worked. For either of them. She wondered where he was. He hated that she didn't trust him. Then he felt guilty for not giving her all the reassurances she wanted, and she felt guilty for needing them in the first place.

But as Derek stared down at Riley, he realized that he was *so* fucked when it came to her if he didn't want to be involved and wrapped up. She was already a part of his life. They had a history. They knew each other's families. He wanted to encourage her in the job with Scott. He wanted her to tell him that his pizza business was a fantastic idea.

And he wanted to fuck her over and over and over again in every position and room in his house.

And he would kind of love it if Riley was the least bit clingy.

And he had no fucking clue how he was going to be able to date Lucy now.

"Yeah, okay, I guess you have a point," he conceded.

She put a hand on his face, and he had to actually hold himself back from saying to hell with it and throwing her over his shoulder anyway. "Yeah, I have a point," she said softly.

He wondered briefly if she was reading some of his thoughts and emotions on his face. He turned his head and kissed her palm. Then he smacked her on the ass and said, "If you don't want to end up bent over on my kitchen table, you better get out of here."

She gave him a smile. "Well, I *do* want that. But I'd still better go."

She bent to retrieve her clothes, and he watched her pull them on. "But you have to say it before you leave, you know," he told her.

Riley pulled her shirt over her head and then lifted her hair out of the back of it. "Say what?"

"You know."

She frowned slightly, but the next moment it was clear she caught on. She smiled and shook her head. "I'm not saying it."

"You have to."

"No way."

"I mean, it's very easy to tell that you think so, but I really think it's only fair you say it."

"I am *not* saying it." But she was grinning.

He moved in close, palmed her ass once more and kissed her. Because he wanted to prove his point.

And because he couldn't help it.

When he lifted his head, she sighed. "Fine. You really *are* a Sex God."

He chuckled at her tone. "Damn right." Then he pinched her and let her go.

"I'll see you later," she told him, blatantly taking another long look at his naked form.

And said form started stirring to life again just from her look.

"See ya." He stood, waiting for her to actually leave.

It was the right thing. She should leave. They couldn't have sex all afternoon. But he certainly wasn't pushing her out the door.

Which should have been the biggest red flag of all.

She sighed and shook her head. "Just wow." Then her eyes finally made it back to his. "See ya 'round."

He laughed. "Yep." No matter if it was complicated or not, there was no avoiding that.

Finally, she turned and headed for his door.

And for the first time in his life, watching that door shut behind a woman made him feel anything but relieved.

"I can't believe you charged him."

Riley sighed as her mother put more green beans on her plate. "Why wouldn't I charge him?"

"He's your brother."

"And he *hired* me to do a job. That he can afford to pay me for," Riley said.

"Do you have any idea how much Kyle gives away to this town?" Erika asked, pulling out her chair and sitting down across from Riley. In the chair she'd sat in for every meal Riley could remember.

"Yes, I have an inkling," Riley said dryly. "But I didn't do his clinic website as a favor, and he's not a charity. I did it because his other designer messed up a bunch of stuff, and he needed some new features added."

For fuck's sake, her mother wanted her to have a job. Now she had one, kind of, and she wasn't supposed to charge for it?

"You don't understand," Erika said, passing the plate of pork chops to her husband. "I guess the computer business is different than health care. But Kyle does a lot of his work for free."

Yes, and he could calm the storms and walk on water. Riley got it. She'd gotten it a long time ago.

"I just thought you could help him out this way and indirectly contribute to the town," Erika added.

"How am I contributing to the town by not charging Kyle for the website?" Riley asked.

"You're helping out the guy who helps so many other people out," Erika said. "Kyle has the money to pay you, of course."

Of course. Because perfect Kyle was far too successful and smart and generous to ever be plagued with not being able to pay his bills.

"But the money he pays you could go to something else. Like that little boy who is having to have some kind of kidney treatment while his dad is deployed. Or Elizabeth Victor," Erika said. "Kyle helped Derek put a ramp in at her house now that she needs a wheelchair when she's out of the house."

Hearing Derek's name made Riley's heart thump in her chest, and she had to resolutely *not* think about it. "But if Kyle already put the ramp in, how does this money help with that?" she asked.

She vaguely realized that she was being a brat. She knew what her mother meant. And she didn't *need* the money. She had no bills, living here with her parents. And she had to be honest—as long as she was in Sapphire Falls, she'd be living with her parents. There weren't a lot of places for rent, and she wasn't buying anything that might signify a commitment to staying.

But there's a really nice couch about nine blocks away. Or even a bed. He invited you into the bed.

She pushed that thought away. She couldn't just keep sleeping on Derek's couch, and she definitely couldn't sleep in his bed on any kind of long-term basis.

Could she?

"You know what I mean," Erika chided as she took a bite.

Riley sighed again and started eating as well. Yeah, she knew what her mom meant. *All* of the things her mom meant. Like that Riley's job could be simply a way of supporting the much more important work her brother was doing.

"I'm working with Scott Hansen on a project for his task force."

Erika looked over as Jake passed the pork chops. "What task force?"

"The sex trafficking task force he works with."

Erika frowned. "Sex trafficking?" She looked concerned. "Why is he doing that?"

Riley set her fork down and leaned in. "Because it's a huge problem, and he's in law enforcement and wants to make a difference."

"But what does he do for that?"

"They go after the people who are trafficking," Riley said. "They find the people doing it, shut them down, arrest them, save the people they've tricked and manipulated and trapped."

She was aware that her voice had risen slightly and that her mother was looking horrified. But that didn't bother Riley. Erika should be horrified. Everyone should be horrified about it.

"Where does he do that?"

"All over the state. The Midwest even," Riley said. "But, Mom, it's happened everywhere. There are local girls affected. Guys too. It's not just females."

"No Sapphire Falls girls have been sex trafficked," Erika said resolutely.

And she was right. "Yet," Riley said.

Her mother's eyes widened. "Don't say that."

"It's true. *Anyone* could be a victim. Even kids from Sapphire Falls."

Erika shook her head. "We would know."

Riley leaned in, but she took a breath before she launched into a rant. Erika wouldn't listen to that. She needed to present the facts calmly and clearly. "These victims don't go into it knowing what's going to happen," she said. "These people use all kinds of things to lure them in. Sometimes it's a call for models or actresses. Sometimes it's job offers—like nanny positions that will allow them to travel to amazing places and see the world. Sometimes they're tricked by someone they meet and get to know and think they can trust."

Erika swallowed. "The kids here don't think about things like modeling or traveling the world."

Riley laughed at that before she could stop herself. "They're kids, Mom. They think the same things that kids in other places do. And yeah, I realize it's never been easy for you to believe, but sometimes people want to leave Sapphire Falls."

"Yes," Erika said coolly. "I'm aware. I've been told many times."

Riley felt a little pang in her chest. Why couldn't her relationship with her mother be easier?

"Well, anyway, I'm working with Scott and the task force," Riley said, bringing the conversation back around. She wanted her mom to know this. She was proud of the fact that she'd been able to help Scott with a couple of the sites. And if she'd introduced a horrible virus to another and flat-out crashed a fourth all on her own, well...everyone knew that technology and the internet could be finicky.

"How are you helping? It's not dangerous is it?" Erika asked.

"I don't want you anywhere around those scumbags," Jake agreed. "You need to be careful."

"I'm nowhere near any of them," Riley said. Though she was already feeling a little urge to volunteer to help Scott more directly. "I'm helping with the computer side of things. They sometimes use websites to attract their victims. I'm helping with taking them down."

Erika looked surprised for a moment. "You mean you're hacking them?"

Riley didn't usually mind the term hacking, but when her mom said it, it came with a whole bunch of judgement. "Yeah, I am."

"So you're helping to take the bad guys down by getting into their websites?"

Riley nodded. "And I'm working on tracking their bank accounts now."

There was a flash of something that almost looked like Erika was impressed. Then she frowned. "Is it legal?"

Riley sighed. "Of course. I'm working with the *cops*."

"Are they paying you?"

"They are," Riley told her. Okay, so those details weren't completely finalized, but Riley was in now. She'd learned enough and already felt enough pride in what she was doing that she was going to keep up with it. And she was going to impress Scott Hansen at least. She was going to become valuable to them. And then she was going to ask them to pay her if they didn't offer. "But I'd do it for free," she added. "I really would. This is important work. I'm helping do something that matters."

Erika gave a slow nod. "Yes. You are."

Riley couldn't believe the sudden jab of relief and happiness she felt in her chest. Should she care what other people thought of her? Maybe not. But she wasn't sure anyone could ever fully shake the idea of wanting their *mothers* to be proud of them.

"And I've been thinking about doing an advocacy and education event here," Riley said, before she could *over*think it and decide not to share. Her mom was very involved in the community and had been a part of arranging a number of community events. She could be a great resource. Especially considering Riley didn't know much about putting those kinds of things together.

"What would that be like?"

"It would be a way to educate the people of Sapphire Falls about sex trafficking and how close to home it can hit and what to be on the lookout for. Peyton and I were also talking about somehow showing victims that Sapphire Falls is a safe place. If they're traveling through and need help, or if they escape and need a place to go..."

"Couldn't that bring some of the sex traffickers to town too?" Erika asked. "If we make a big deal about it, they might decide to come here to look for girls."

Riley frowned. "Sex traffickers could already be coming through town," she said. "They could be gassing up at The Stop. They could be eating at the diner or getting a drink at the Come Again. We can't build a fence or a bubble around Sapphire Falls."

Though from everything she'd heard, Scott was trying his best to keep watch over every inch of the town. Partly because of his work with the task force. He knew how normal the people involved in the dirty, horrible world of sex trafficking could look and how easily the victims could fall prey.

"Don't say that," Erika told her.

"Not saying it doesn't make it less true," Riley said, barely resisting her eye roll.

They all ate quietly for a couple of minutes.

Then Erika said, "You know, I'm sure your brother has worked with sexual abuse victims."

Riley swallowed. Yeah, she was sure he had. And she was sure he was good at it. Kyle was calm and reassuring and could even be funny and charming if needed. He was also a damned good doctor. She nodded. "I'm sure he has."

"Have you asked him about any of this? Maybe to get involved?"

Riley pressed her lips together. She hadn't. Not because he wouldn't be great at it, but because... She wasn't sure. She supposed she thought maybe the ultimate advocacy project would involve a lot of people, a committee or something, and she was not the kind of person to head up something like that. She guessed that Scott would do it. Maybe. Or Peyton. Not that Peyton was any more the committee chair type than Riley was.

She set her fork down and decided to be honest with herself first. She hadn't asked Kyle because she kind of wanted to do something great that didn't involve him.

Then she decided to be honest with her mother. "Kyle doesn't have to be a part of *everything* in this town."

Erika opened her mouth to reply when they heard the front door open and, "Hey, anyone home?"

Speak of the devil.

Kyle came into the kitchen with a big grin and a huge cake in one hand, and Hannah's hand in the other.

"Hi, honey." Erika pushed back from the table and went to take the cake from him.

"Are we in time to have dessert?" Kyle asked. He slapped his dad's shoulder while Hannah leaned over and kissed Jake's cheek.

"Hey, Riley," Hannah greeted.

"Hi." Riley really liked Hannah. She made Kyle happy, and it was clearly mutual. All through high school, Hannah had been a fixture at this kitchen table. She and Kyle had been inseparable. They'd broken up for a few years, and Riley knew that Kyle had tried to get over her. But Hannah had only been back in Sapphire Falls for a few days before they'd gotten back together. And Riley could honestly say that Kyle had relaxed since Hannah had been back. He smiled more. He joked more. He took more time off. Not that he was ever completely off. He was the only doctor in town. But he didn't go looking for jobs and activities all over town like he'd once done. Like Derek did now.

And just that easily, Derek Wright was back in her head. Did Derek keep himself so busy because he didn't have any reason to stay home? And if she'd said yes to staying in bed all day, would he have really blown off all the odd jobs she was sure he had lined up? And would he really be able to blow them off on a regular basis once he had a girlfriend?

And why did she suddenly *hate* the idea of him having a girlfriend?

Riley forced her thoughts back to the conversation happening around her. About the education and advocacy program that she'd just told her parents about. The conversation that went on without her, with Kyle and Hannah both inputting what they knew and getting excited about helping.

Riley sat back in her chair feeling disappointed and suddenly left out. Of something *she'd* brought up. Dammit.

Her phone vibrated in her pocket, and she suddenly prayed it was someone whose computer had crashed and needed help immediately. She didn't want to play IT guy to the entire town and yet...it beat having dinner and dessert with her family at the moment.

But it wasn't a computer crash.

It was Derek. And her stupid heart did a stupid flip.

You know, you could come down early to taste test the pizza.

Pizza. Now there was something that was *always* a good idea. And Derek. Who had recently become one of her favorite ideas. Oh boy.

I'd actually love that. But might be a bit. Kind of in the middle of something.

Kyle and Hannah there?

Yes. How did you know?

He mentioned it.

Ah.

But I will see you later?

Hope so.

She did want to get out of here, but she was also aware that if she left in the middle of this conversation, it would look like she didn't really care about the topic. And God only knew what her family would come up with without her. They'd have the entire program planned. And very likely she'd be left out of it completely.

Ten minutes later, Riley had put her foot down twice—about a program and event that she'd only *just* begun having the tiniest inkling about yesterday—and she had four pages of written notes that she planned to run past Peyton. She wasn't sure how this whole thing had snowballed on her, but that would teach her to open her mouth to try to impress her mother.

Then again, some of these ideas were really good.

But she was now really ready for some pizza. Or some Derek. She wasn't sure which, but pizza seemed like a safer thing to be craving.

The doorbell rang, and she nearly sagged with relief at the interruption. "Okay, this is all good, but I have to talk to Scott," she said. Scott, who hadn't exactly *hired* her for the job. The job that she wasn't even sure technically existed. But she was going to have to make it exist. Or maybe she'd do this all voluntarily. But either way, *she* was going to do it.

"I'll get it," Jake said, pushing his chair back.

Riley took the opportunity to get up too. She was going to get pizza. This was enough family time for now.

But as she gathered her papers and her mom started picking up the dishes from the table, her dad came back into the room. "Hey, everyone. Derek's here."

Riley's head came up fast, and her gaze collided with Derek's the moment he rounded the corner. As if he'd been looking for her first.

"Derek." Erika was clearly thrilled to see him. "Hi, honey. Do you want some cake?"

"Hi, Erika." He crossed to her and dropped a quick kiss on her cheek. "Nope, I just dropped by to pick Riley up."

Riley felt surprise jolt through her. He looked over at her

and winked, and she covered her shock. "Oh, is it time already?"

"Pick Riley up?" Erika asked.

"Yeah, she's taste testing some of my pizzas tonight for me."

Erika looked at Riley. "You didn't say anything. You didn't have to eat with us if you promised to help Derek."

Which Riley decoded to mean, "If you have a chance to hang out with Derek, you should take it because he's amazing." And he kind of was.

"I'm always happy to taste pizza," Riley's dad joked.

Derek laughed easily. "Oh, don't worry. I'll be asking you all what you think. But I have to start with Riley."

"Oh?" Erika asked.

"Yep," Derek said. "I haven't quite been able to convince Riley that I can do no wrong like I have you." Derek put an arm around Erika's shoulders and gave her a smile. "I need her brutal honestly here at the start."

Erika squeezed him. "Well, it's hard not to think that." She returned his smile, then focused on Riley. "You'll be nice though, right?"

And it suddenly hit Riley that she could *not* date Derek. No matter what. Not that it was on the table or even the remotest possibility, but she couldn't date him. Her mother would *never* think she was doing that right. If Riley couldn't even become a sex trafficking victim's advocate without her mom thinking she needed help, there was no way she could be in a relationship— something she was not all that great at to date—with one of her mother's favorite people in the world without her thinking Riley wasn't doing it right. God forbid they ever have an argument. Or break up.

"I'll be honest," Riley said. But good Lord, at this moment, she *loved* him for showing up like this. "But yes, I'll be nice."

"You just have a tendency to be a little blunt," Erika said.

Riley opened her mouth to reply, but Derek beat her to it. "That's one thing I love about her."

Whoa. That was...*what*?

"I also love that she's always up for trying new stuff, that she can hack the shit out of any computer system, and that she never apologizes for just being her." He gave her a grin, and Riley felt her panties get a little warm. "If Riley likes something, you know it and can truly bet on it being awesome."

Yeah, whoa. Just...whoa. He loved things about her? Things that drove her mom crazy? And he was willing to say that *to* her mom?

"Don't you think it's awesome that you can always depend on Riley to make you think about new things you haven't thought about before and old things in a different way?" he asked, directing the question at Erika.

Riley realized she was holding her breath.

Her mother was studying her with a puzzled look on her face. After a long moment, she nodded. "I guess she does do that."

Riley couldn't have been more surprised if her mother had announced she was going to get a few tattoos to match Riley's.

There was a long, totally silent pause. Then her brother, shockingly, said, "Yeah, me too." He gave Riley a grin. "And if Riley says Derek's pizza is good, everyone will know that's the God's honest truth."

That was nice. It wasn't that Riley didn't think her brother loved her. She knew that her inability to be on time for things and her messy bedroom and her general disregard for most rules drove him crazy. But she'd always gotten the impression that Kyle understood why she did the things she did. All her unorganized, don't-care attitude had been on purpose. She was actually quite on top of things with her work and, while her apartment in California wasn't immaculate, it wasn't the mess her high school bedroom had been.

But it was nice to hear Kyle say some things he appreciated about her too. And that it was her honesty that people most liked.

And if I say Derek's good boyfriend material, all the women in town will know that's the God's honest truth.

She could do that. She *would* do that. He was a good guy. Who she couldn't have.

But she felt her freaking bottom lip tremble.

Coincidentally, that was the moment Derek let her mom go, took three steps toward her, and held out his hand. "So, let's go already. I can't wait to see what you think."

She didn't look at her parents or her brother as she reached out, took his hand, and let him tug her out of the kitchen.

He kept going down the hall toward the front door.

"Who's covering the bar?" she asked, the realization that he showed up here when he should have been at work just occurring to her.

"I'm not the only one who can pour beer in this town. I'm just the only one *willing* to stay up until midnight doing it every night." He shot her a quick grin.

For some reason, her stomach flipped.

"So who's babysitting the bar while you run over here?"

He pulled the front door open. "Bryan. Until midnight. Then he's closing up."

"The bar is closing at midnight?"

"Yep." He gestured for her to step out of the door.

"But what about the people who all come in after midnight?"

"They'll be okay."

She still hadn't stepped out of the door. She turned to face him fully, standing closer than she really needed to for the conversation. But he'd rescued her in there. And she wanted to stand close to him. Really close. "Why aren't you going to be at work tonight?"

"I have somewhere else to be."

"Where?"

"With you."

That made her feel a rush of warmth and affection. Was that what *he* was feeling? Or was he feeling sorry for her? Or horny? "Why?"

He let out a breath. "Ry, do you really want to talk about that? I mean, we can delve in, if you want, but I think that might be more than either of us is really up to right now."

He had a point. A very good point. This was complicated. And that meant he wasn't just horny or feeling sorry for her. "Are we going to eat pizza?"

"Maybe."

"But that's important to you."

He looked down at her. "Yeah. That's one thing that's important to me."

Oh, boy. They didn't even need to actually talk about anything for this to be complicated.

"You'll have to cook the pizzas in the oven at the bar for them to taste right."

He nodded.

"So eventually, we'll end up there."

"Eventually."

"Okay." She took a breath. "But let's not go straight over there."

"Where do you want to go instead?"

That was a no-brainer. The warmth and affection contributed to *her* feeling horny. But a second later she corrected that. It wasn't horny. Exactly. She just wanted to be close to him. As close as she could get. "Somewhere where no one will look for us. And that we can be naked for a while."

His gaze heated and he nodded. But he didn't seem completely surprised. "I really do like it when you're blunt."

Yeah, he'd even told her mom that.

And Riley wanted to climb on top of him and lose herself in pleasure with a guy who not only really knew her, but appreciated some of her more annoying characteristics.

They drove out to the river. She knew that's where he was headed the minute he turned out of town. And it was the perfect choice. No one would look for them to be there together, alone.

Once they had bumped over the narrow dirt road that led down to the river, he turned east and continued along the bank for a few hundred feet. The dirt road ended at the best place to park and carry coolers down to the sand right along the edge of the river. It was the most popular party spot. It was also a spot that was likely to have other visitors at some time tonight. Instead, Derek turned and drove over the grass, heading west, and parked two football-field lengths away. He backed the truck up to the edge of the short bluff that overlooked the river and killed the engine.

9

———

"**Y**ou okay?"

She turned on the seat to face him. She nodded. "I'm just kind of overwhelmed with wanting to screw your brains out as a thank-you for sticking up for me with my family."

He gave her a slow smile. "Overwhelmed?"

"I've never felt that before."

He frowned. "You've never had someone stick up for you before?"

She shook her head. "I've never wanted someone…" But she trailed off and frowned too. "I'm not sure I have, actually."

"Ry—"

"My family isn't abusive or anything," she said quickly. "I don't think I could make a case at all for having a rough childhood. My mom's just…" She shrugged. "Critical. She has high standards. We butt heads. But I know she loves me and I love her and…I'm fine. It's just that I've never had anyone say that my flaws are something they like about me."

Derek stretched his arm across the back of the seat. He tugged on the end of the strand of hair that lay against her shoulder. "They're not flaws."

She shrugged her other shoulder because she didn't want to dislodge his touch. "My bluntness and my seeming inability to do anything traditionally definitely drive people crazy."

"They drive your mom crazy," he agreed. "But they're not flaws."

She took a breath, feeling more than just her panties getting warmer now. The sweet side of Derek was as addictive as the hot and cocky side. "Thanks."

"That doesn't mean you don't have flaws. Those just aren't them."

Ah, and there was the guy she knew. But she grinned. "Oh?"

"Yeah." He rotated his finger and wrapped the end of her hair around it. "For one, you don't listen very well."

"I don't?"

"The minute your mom starts talking, you start thinking of all the things she's saying that are wrong and critical. You don't hear the other stuff."

Riley arched her brows. Oh, okay, so this was kind of serious. "Is that right?"

He nodded. "It is. She's on your ass a lot, I'll agree, but you don't hear her saying things like 'I worry about you', 'I want you to be happy', 'I want you to make good choices and not just pick the option I'll hate the most'."

Riley frowned now. "She doesn't say that stuff."

"She does. It's between the lines, and yeah, it's mixed up with 'do you really think you should dye your hair?' and 'you could do more with your life,' but it's there."

"Well, that other stuff is way louder and more in focus," Riley said, feeling her chest tighten.

Derek nodded again. "I know. But you've done some dumb stuff, Ry. And she's your mom. Of course she's going to worry."

"Hey."

He shrugged, unapologetic. "One of the things we have going for us is that we can *both* be brutally honest, right?"

"You mean, you want permission to keep teasing me about shit like you've always done."

He thought about that for a second. Then nodded, a small smile curling his lips. "Yeah. I guess so. I know it's pretty easy to fall under my spell when I'm doling out multiple orgasms, but I don't want you to get soft. I want to be able to tell you when you're being a brat."

How had talking about sex gotten so easy so fast with this guy?

But things had always been pretty easy with Derek. Because she'd never cared what he thought.

In the next second, Riley realized that wasn't true at all. She'd cared. She just hadn't *worried*. There was something about Derek, about him always being there, about him being such a solid fixture in her life, that she'd never worried about him getting offended or sick of her. She could be herself, tell him what she thought, do her own thing even knowing he'd tease her, because she knew he'd always be there. Even when she didn't think she wanted him to be.

She needed a guy like that.

That realization hit hard and direct. She wanted to be able to do her own thing, do things differently, try new stuff, take a few risks, and she needed someone who would be honest with her—not critical like her mom, but just honest—and who would encourage her to try those things, and be there even when she made the wrong choice or did something stupid. She needed the freedom to be herself that came from knowing there was someone—or multiple someones—who'd be there anyway.

And Derek was one of those people.

He was maybe the main person. Based on tonight, when he was the one to point out that those things could also be kind of great.

"You can keep telling me when I'm being a brat," she told

him. Then she started to lean in, because she really did want to screw his brains out.

"Hang on." He put a hand up—right on her forehead, keeping her from moving closer.

She frowned and sat back. "What?"

"When you come over here, you need to have lost the pants," he said, pointing at her jeans.

Oh, that was easy. She started to unbutton.

"And," he added, "I have one more thing to say first."

She sighed and paused with her zipper halfway down. "What?"

"I stuck up for you tonight because you needed it, and everything I said was true and I wanted your family to hear me say it."

She waited, hearing a "but" coming.

"But," he went on, "I will also say to *you* that your brother is a great guy. One of the best. He might be a little uptight about schedules and things, but he never stops. He never stops caring and working and wondering what else he could do. And I don't like the idea that your sole purpose in life is to be the opposite of him."

She stared at Derek. Okay, she knew the annoying tease, the cocky flirt, the sweet friend sides of him. But she wasn't sure she'd seen the staunch defender before. First *for* her, and now *to* her.

"I know Kyle is a great guy."

"I know you do."

"But you want me to be nicer to him? More respectful? What?"

"Yes. I mean, basically all of that. You don't need to be the opposite of him in every way," Derek said.

Riley took a breath. Fair enough. "You think I'm insulting him somehow?"

"I think you used to," Derek said. "But no, that's not what I mean. I think you're missing out on some of the ways for *you* to be happy and even more amazing just because you're so determined to not follow in his footsteps."

Riley just looked at him. Wow. Derek really did know her. And he got her family dynamic. And he was willing and able to be fully honest with her. And he wanted her to be... She frowned.

"Why does this all matter to you?"

He frowned back. "Really?"

"I'm just wondering. You seem to want to fix some things for me. Why does it matter to you?"

"Jesus, Riley," he said, clearly annoyed. "You don't know?"

"Just tell me."

"Because I care about you. I want you to be happy. And I think you'll be happy if you can really throw yourself into the advocacy stuff and the computer work for the task force, and if you can come to a place where you and your mom can talk about all of it without you getting defensive."

Her breath caught in her throat. She licked her lips. Then she asked a question that she already knew the answer to but wanted to hear out loud. "Because you want me to change? You want me to give up some of the rebellion and be more like everyone else in Sapphire Falls."

"Fuck no," he said, scowling. "You'll never be like everyone else in Sapphire Falls anyway. But, no. I want you to be happy. If I thought you really were, that the rebellious thing and living far away and working for big companies really did that for you, then it would be great. But you've been looking for something —for a long time. Like maybe since you were in high school. And I think you've been looking for a way to contribute and be a part of something that matters and be close to your family, without losing out on being your own person. I want *that* for you."

Yep, that was what she'd wanted to hear out loud. Because

she was quickly realizing that having Derek Wright know her and get her, and want her anyway, was a really, really huge turn-on.

"You want me to be more like you."

He frowned, and blinked, and frowned again. "What?"

"You have all of that. You contribute and are a part of something and are close to your family—and everyone else here. But you're your own person."

He must have realized how close she'd gotten, because his gaze dropped to her lips. "Am I?" he asked.

She hadn't expected that. She paused. "Are you what?"

"My own person. Or am I just like everyone else who never got out of this town? Am I fooling myself into thinking that opening a pizza business will somehow save me from looking back someday and wondering what else I could have done? I mean, I'm thinking about seriously dating someone now just because my friends are settling down. How is that being my own person?"

Riley had never, in all the years she'd known him, seen Derek Wright vulnerable. And it was doing something to her insides that she couldn't explain. She knew somehow that he'd never said this stuff to Kyle or Scott. But he was saying it to her.

And one of the things he liked—no, *loved*; he'd said loved—about her was that she was honest with him.

"Are you happy?" she asked him.

He met her gaze directly. "Yeah. Overall."

"And can you imagine doing anything else? Teaching? Being a lawyer or a dentist or flying airplanes or farming?" she asked.

He shook his head. "No."

"Because you don't think you'd be good at any of that? Or smart enough? Or dedicated enough?"

"Because I don't want to do anything else."

She smiled, feeling strangely triumphant and happy. For

him. "So you're happy doing exactly what you want to be doing."

He took a breath. "Yeah."

"Derek, the only reason that feels weird sometimes when you look around, is because very few people get to that point this early in life. Some never do. You did. And frankly—" She thought only for a millisecond about not admitting this to him. "I'm jealous of that." Then she said something she'd *never* imagined saying to Derek. "And you're right. About me. I've been restless for a long time because I've been telling myself to be one way, while my heart's been telling me that's not right."

He ran a hand down her arm. "Don't tell me you think these tattoos are wrong. Because these are hotter than hell."

She smiled, looking down at the intricate swirls that covered her arm. "No. Not those things. The tattoos and the hair and the piercings and the computer stuff...that's all me." It might have started as a rebel-against-her-mother thing, but she'd quickly realized that expressing herself that way was very satisfying. "But," she met his eyes again, "I don't want to work for corporations or banks. I think computer and tech work for law enforcement is right up my alley."

He grinned. "You just started that."

But she knew he wasn't disagreeing with her. She nodded. "Yeah, well, when something feels right, I think it's very possible to know right away."

Their gazes held, and they seemed to be agreeing silently. And not just about her computer work.

"You're going to make amazing pizza, you know that?"

"Yeah, well, it's just pizza."

"Nothing you do is *just* anything, Derek," she said, sincerely. "You put your heart into the things you do for this town. This will be the same."

He nodded. "Which means if it fails, it will hurt more."

Riley was thrilled with how he was opening up to her. "So don't fail."

He gave her a grin. "It's that easy?"

She shook her head. "No. But I'll be telling you you're screwing something up long before it becomes a true failure. You'll have a chance to fix it and make it right. And I know you'll keep working until it's perfect. Don't worry."

He snorted at that. But when he said, "Thanks," in a husky, almost emotional voice, she felt her own smile fade.

And a sudden intense desire take its place.

"Hey, Ry?" he asked after a moment.

"Yeah?"

"Why don't you take your pants off and come over here now?"

Gladly. She unzipped and pushed everything off and to the floor of the truck. He was watching her with hot eyes as she crawled over the seat to him. She paused to unzip him as well, and he didn't move to stop her. He just gave a heartfelt groan as she freed his cock and gave it a long stroke.

"Shirt too. The moon is nice and bright tonight," he told her.

It sure was. She could see his hard length clearly with the light shining through the windshield. She didn't think, just stripped her shirt off and unhooked her bra. But before he could touch her, she took him in hand again and leaned over.

The first touch of her mouth to the head of his cock had him tangling his hands in her hair and his breath hissing out.

She took him deep, then dragged her lips back up his length. "How are you this hard already?" she asked, looking up at him.

He was watching her with a hot intensity that made her tingle from head to toe.

"Guess I like pizza a lot."

She laughed, and she felt his fingers tighten in her hair. "I will definitely keep that in mind when we do the taste testing."

"Yeah, I'm thinking of some other things I'd like to taste right now." His voice had that delicious, low gruffness to it.

"Too bad the front seat of a pickup is a lot more conducive to blowjobs than to...that." She gave his head a little lick.

"That sounds like a dare," he told her, doing nothing to discourage her from taking his length in nice and slow, and then coming back up with her tongue sliding along the underside.

"Oh, I have no doubt that you could get it done." In fact, she had no doubt he'd gotten it done, very well, in the past. With other girls. "But I'm pretty happy right here."

"You don't want me to make you come on my tongue?"

Her whole body clenched. She gave him a long, hard suck, just to remind him that she was busy. "You really want me to stop?"

"Hell no."

"Well then..."

Somehow—and she would spend time later that night replaying it and trying to figure out how he'd done it so quickly and smoothly—Derek grabbed her, turned them both, and settled her right over his mouth. He gave her a long, deep lick and a suck, and she completely forgot to care about how he got her there, only that he'd *keep* her there for a while.

"**D**erek," she moaned.

His body got even tighter and hotter as he heard his name on her lips. "Damn, I love hearing my name like that," he said from between her legs.

He might have had other girls in his pickup with their pants off, but he'd never brought anyone to the river, just the two of them. He'd gone to parties with other women. He'd gone *home* from parties with other women. But he'd never had sex here. He supposed because he didn't have to. He had a bed. They all had beds. Why would he bring them to the river? He didn't need to romance them. He didn't need to be sure that no one could find them. Sure, he was disappointed if someone got a phone call and had to leave before he got her bra off. But he'd never died from it.

With Riley, he swore that if he didn't make love to her out here tonight, he would die. His heart would actually stop beating.

And was that completely dramatic and out of character for him? Yes, it was.

That didn't make it feel less true.

He licked up over her clit and relished the way she tightened her knees against his ears and the sharp intake of air.

"Holy—" She ended the thought with a gasp as he swirled his tongue over her clit. "*Yes.*"

He loved hearing his effect on her. He loved feeling it and tasting it too. He could happily spend the next two hours right here, doing this. But he needed her mouth on his cock.

"You know, the beauty of this position is we can both do it at the same time," he said. He gave her butt a little swat.

"Right. Sorry."

He started to say something sarcastic, but she immediately took his cock in hand and slid her mouth down over his length.

His groan felt like it came from his bones. *Nothing* had ever felt like this. Yes, fucking her against the wall had been amazing. He wanted to do that a few hundred more times. But this... something about having her spread out over his mouth while she took him deep in hers felt different. It was dirty and intimate and so unlike anything he'd ever imagined with this girl that he couldn't quite get over it.

He hung on for a few minutes, feasting on her, letting the

feel of her hot, sassy mouth taking him in over and over wash through him. But he couldn't take it for long. He gripped her hips and rotated her as he sat up, swinging her around until she was straddling his thighs. Thank God his seat went *way* back.

"That," he kissed her deep and hard, "is what happens when you dare me."

"I'll definitely keep that in mind," she said breathlessly.

"But this…" He lifted her slightly, brought her forward and then down. She sank down onto his cock, and the happy sigh she gave made his balls tighten. "Is what happens when you're amazing and sweet and brutally honest and bratty and gorgeous."

"I can keep a couple of those up for sure."

He laughed. She could keep all of those going—and he was never going to get over her.

The thought seemed to come out of nowhere, but before he could give it more attention, she wrapped her arms around his neck, pressed her lips to his, and said, "Okay, Sex God, let's do this thing."

And they did. His hands gripped her hips as he moved her up and down, and while she helped lift and lower her body on his, he set the pace, he controlled how deep he thrust, and he was the one to finally say, "Come for me, Ry. Please come for me."

She called out his name as her body clenched around him, and he felt like the god she teased him about being. He really fucking did. Because Riley Ames didn't do anything anyone told her to do.

He thrust up into her sweet, hot body. Her tightness gripped him and he wrapped his arms around her, holding her close as he hammered his hips upward. He felt the orgasm bearing down and he let go with a shout. Her name. He couldn't help but shout her name.

She slumped against him, and he just held her. They

breathed together for several long minutes, and Derek realized that he didn't have one iota of anxiety about getting back to the bar, about any other project, about his pizzas. Holding this woman was exactly where he wanted to be.

So when her phone rang in the pocket of her jeans on the floor of his truck, he swore.

She pulled back and smiled at him. "I'm flattered."

"Don't answer it."

"I have to."

"Someone wants something."

"Probably."

He squeezed her ass. "Well, there's no one who wants more from you than I do."

He felt her tense up, saw her eyes go wide, and realized what he'd said. He thought about it quickly. Should he joke about it? Tease her about assuming too much?

But she wasn't assuming too much. He wasn't joking. He wanted her. All of her. He wanted her to stay in Sapphire Falls. He wanted her to work with Scott. He wanted her to be at the Come Again with him every night he worked. And he wanted to work fewer nights. He wanted to take time off. He wanted to stay home.

"Riley—"

"I have to answer it." She slid off his lap and reached for her pants. She looked at the number, then swiped the screen to answer it. "Hi."

She listened for a moment, then her eyes got big—even bigger than when Derek had basically admitted he was falling for her—and she said, "Yes, of course. Oh my God."

She disconnected and started pulling her clothes on.

"What's wrong?"

She jerked her T-shirt over her head. "Nothing. Exactly. Scott needs me to help him with something."

"That was *Scott*?" He was going to strangle his friend.

"Yeah. He's working on something. Three girls have disappeared from Lincoln, but they think they have a way to track them. They need me."

Derek felt his chest tighten. Fuck. Three girls had disappeared? That...yeah, if Riley could do anything about it, she had to go.

He yanked his pants up and zipped and buttoned. Then he started the truck. But he paused with his hand on the gearshift.

"Ry, I—" What was he going to say? *I had a great time? I never want to stop fucking you? Come over after you're done with work? I want to make you breakfast in the morning?*

All things women had said to *him* after sex. All things that had felt clingy and unnecessary. All things he really wanted to say right now.

"Are you going to Lincoln?" he asked. *God, be careful. Call me when you get there. Maybe I should come along.*

He ran a hand over his face. He needed to snap out of this.

"I don't know," she said. "Scott asked if I could meet him at the station."

Maybe she would just be working from here. That was one thing about all this cyber stuff. She could do it remotely at least. But instead of telling her that he really wanted to see her after she was done, whenever that was, he just put the truck into drive and started back down the dirt road.

They didn't talk on the way to town, and by the time he pulled up in front of the station, he'd realized that he couldn't say any of the things that were rolling through his head. The best thing about him and Riley was that they were him and Riley, with sex added in. He didn't want any of that to change.

"So, try not to get arrested, okay?" he said as she opened the door.

She shot him a grin. "You good for bail money if I do?"

Thank God they were grinning and teasing. "Yeah. But the interest rates on my loan would be really high," he told her.

"Oh, yeah? What percent are we talking here?"

"Let's just say there will be handcuffs involved on *that* end of the situation as well."

She laughed. "Now I almost hope I *do* need bail money."

She slid out of the truck and had just started to close the door when, stupidly, Derek said, "Ry."

She stopped and looked in at him. "Yeah?"

"Call me. Later. Whenever."

She chewed on her bottom lip for a moment, and he was certain that she was thinking of a good way to say no, that was a bad idea. But instead, she nodded, "I will."

"Okay."

She slammed the door, and he watched her walk up to the front of the police station and go inside. He blew out a breath. Fuck.

He pulled out his phone and texted Scott. *You better take care of her. This shit better not be dangerous.*

He waited nearly three minutes with no response. He was tempted to stick around and wait to see if Riley and Scott came back out and left. Of course, then he probably would have followed them, and *that* would have been pathetic.

Right.

He drove home, absolutely unable to come up with a thing to do. Or at least not anything he wanted to do. He could go back to the Come Again and let Bryan go home. But he didn't really want to wait on people tonight. He could swing by his grandma's house. She'd probably bake him brownies while he took a look at the wiring in the dishwasher. But he didn't want to work on a dishwasher tonight. Or eat brownies.

And *that* was absolutely pathetic.

His phone finally pinged with a message. *She'll be fine* was Scott's answer.

It wasn't good enough.

Dammit. What do you have her doing? Where is she going?

Scott's answer a moment later was, *Who is this and why do you have Derek's phone?*

Ha, ha. Fucking hilarious. *Don't make me come down there.* He looked at the words that he didn't think he'd ever actually say to anyone about anything, but he pushed send anyway. He wasn't the possessive type. He just never got that worked up. None of the stuff he had couldn't be replaced. None of the women in his life were ever supposed to stay.

Until now.

So come down here. She's working right here in the station. I'm sure she'd love to have you breathing down her neck.

Derek wished Scott was actually here, because he'd love to tell him to fuck off in person.

What the hell is going on with you? Scott asked.

Well, that was a really good question. *Nothing.*

Bullshit.

Seriously. Just want to be sure this new thing is safe for Riley.

Because?

Because I want her to be okay.

I'm here. And she's doing what she's best at.

Yeah. But... He quickly deleted the words. Scott was right. Riley was fine. And it was none of his business.

Never mind, he finally typed.

Scott was right on that reply too. *Yeah, sure, I'll just never mind that you're in love with Riley.*

Derek read the words over again. And tried to figure out why they didn't shock him. But he'd been the one to help both Scott and Kyle see how they really felt about Peyton and Hannah.

He thought about typing *don't tell her*, but he knew Scott wouldn't. He also knew that as of right this minute, Scott was going to give him shit the next time he saw him. So he did go ahead and type, *Just take care of her.*

At least he left off the *for me* he was tempted to include.

Then he stomped in the house, popped a beer, and turned on the television. And brooded until it was time to go to bed. He hadn't gotten a text from Riley, but he also hadn't sent Riley any texts checking up on her. That was something.

But now it was midnight, and he hadn't heard from her and...fuck it.

He texted *I want you*. He hit send. Then shut his light off.

Fifteen minutes later, he didn't have a text back. But he heard his front door open, the creak of someone walking over the floorboards in the hall. Riley slipped into his room, kicked her shoes off, and shed her clothes down to her panties. Derek lifted the blanket, and she slid underneath and right up against him.

Feeling an incredible sense of happiness, he wrapped his arm around her and put his nose in her hair.

"You okay?" he asked against the back of her neck.

"They found the girls," she said quietly. "But they were really shaken up."

He felt a tremor go through her. "You too, Ry?"

"Yeah."

He tightened his hold on her, tucking her more firmly under his chin. She took a big, deep breath, then let it out. Her body stopped shaking and she finally turned to face him. She wrapped her arms around him and snuggled close.

Her naked breasts pressed into his chest, but all he could think about was that she was here. She'd come to him when she was feeling shaken. That seemed right. And amazing.

"How can I help?" he asked.

"Can I stay over? I don't want to sleep alone in the basement."

He opened his mouth, but before he could reply, she said, "And can you tease me a little bit or something? Like call me a wuss for needing to be held or something. I just don't want anything else serious tonight."

Yeah, it didn't get a lot more serious than sex trafficking. He wanted to tell her that he was proud of her. He wanted to point out that she'd helped save lives tonight. He wanted to ask about what all had gone down, honestly. But that wasn't what she needed from him.

So he ran his hand across her lower back and said, "Damn. I really am amazing. I'm going to sleep all night with a half-naked woman who I want more than anything, and all I'm going to do is hold her."

Okay that wasn't the best teasing he'd ever done, but hopefully it would work.

She wiggled a little. "Do you want me to put a shirt on?"

"I most definitely do *not* want you to put a shirt on."

She turned again, so her butt was against his cock. "So you'll be okay?"

In spite of the position, and how much his cock liked it Derek could hear the smile in her voice, and he felt a knot of tension ease in his shoulders. "Yeah. But I'll probably deserve a reward in the morning."

"Do you like chocolate chips?" she asked.

"I think I could come up with a few ways to incorporate chocolate chips, yes." He nuzzled her hair.

"Well, it's not hard," she said. "You just mix them into the pancake batter."

"Ah, chocolate chip pancakes," he said. "*That's* my reward?"

"Yes."

He was pretty sure he could change her mind about that.

"After we have sex in your shower."

That was more like it. "Fair warning, I have a loofah and I'm not afraid to use it."

She wiggled again, and he heard a soft giggle. He wasn't sure he'd ever felt better.

"'Night, Ry," he said, kissing the top of her head.

She gave another of those soft, happy sighs. "'Night, Derek."

He waited a few seconds, then he said softly, "And if you wake me up before eight a.m. tomorrow, I *will* spank your ass."

His hand was resting on her stomach, and he felt the little hitch in her breathing.

"Not sure that's the deterrent that you think it is," she replied.

He grinned. "Okay, how about this...I'll spank you for letting me sleep past nine."

She covered his hand with hers. "Deal."

10

———

They slept 'til 10:08. Or at least Riley did. She blinked at the clock on Derek's bedside table. He clearly had light-blocking curtains on his windows because his room was still gloriously dark even though it was halfway through the morning.

Riley stretched, rolling onto her back, feeling well rested, completely satisfied, and pretty damned happy.

Last night had been intense. Good, but intense. She'd helped the cops track the girls to a rundown hotel on the outskirts of Chicago. They'd not only found the three from Lincoln, but four other girls. Five guys were in custody, and the hotel owner was being questioned.

She'd felt good about the work and ecstatic for the outcome. But it had also been draining. Those five guys, those seven girls, were just a drop in a huge bucket, and while she was fully dedicated to do everything she could now, it was depressing that there was so much work to be done.

Riley hadn't been shocked to find herself on Derek's porch afterward. She hadn't been surprised to find his front door unlocked either. And she hadn't been surprised by how good it felt to slip into bed beside him and ask him to hold her.

He'd done a great job of it. She hadn't slept that hard in a long time.

And now it was late in the morning and she was...alone.

She looked over at the other side of the bed. And frowned. What about the shower sex?

Swinging her legs over the side of the bed, Riley ran her fingers through her hair and looked around. She spotted one of Derek's T-shirts flung over the chair in the corner. She grabbed it, pulling it on as she headed out of the bedroom.

But he was not just missing from the bed. He wasn't in the house at all. And there was no coffee brewing or breakfast being made. No chocolate chip pancakes for sure.

Okay, so she didn't need to know where he was or what he was doing. It was sweet that he'd let her sleep. Shower sex would have been great, but they could do that when he got back from wherever he was. It wasn't a big deal. She just kind of wanted to *know* where he was.

She started the coffee and headed into the living room to grab her phone from her purse. She had a text, but it was from Peyton, not Derek.

Heard you were kick-ass last night. Thank you!

Riley smiled. She *had* been kick-ass last night. It had really, overall, been awesome. And it had truly energized her to get the education and advocacy program off the ground.

In fact, she had a little time now. Might as well work on some ideas.

It was a great excuse to kill time at Derek's house. It wouldn't look like she was stalling so she could see him. Probably.

She settled down at the table with her computer and a cup of coffee. It was nice here. Quiet. The sun lit the kitchen up this time of day, and she found it soothing and easy to concentrate.

So much so that she didn't hear Derek come in until he walked into the kitchen and came up short in the doorway.

"Oh, hey."

She looked up quickly. "Hey." But her smile died. He looked surprised to see her. As if he hadn't expected her to still be here. "I was…" She gestured at her computer. "I was just getting some work done on the sex trafficking program."

He nodded and moved toward the coffeepot. He was wearing jeans and a dark blue T-shirt. Both were streaked with mud.

"What have you been up to?"

He turned with his full cup and a slight frown. "Got a call. Kind of early. Didn't want to wake you."

She gave him a little smile. "I wasn't shy about waking you the past few mornings."

He tipped his head in acknowledgement. "But we both know I'm a nicer guy than you."

"Indeed. I've never been much of a guy at all."

The corner of his mouth curled. "I noticed."

"Not until recently."

"Oh, way back. I ogled you good a few times."

This was good. It was kind of banter-y. And she did like the idea of him ogling her. "Yeah? Well, ditto."

He chuckled at that. "You never ogled me."

"Oh, really? I particularly liked the neon-green swim trunks you had that one summer."

That had been about six years ago. Had she really ogled him that far back? But she had to admit, she'd learned firsthand from Derek Wright that six-pack abs and that awesome V guys had on either side of those abs could be real.

Derek set his cup down and braced his hands on the counter on either side of his hips. "That was a long time ago."

"Yeah." She knew that she looked a little puzzled by that too.

"I guess the not-liking-me thing kept you from doing anything about it anyway."

Her gaze flew to his face. "What not-liking-you thing?"

"You didn't like me." He shrugged. "I was like an annoying brother who wasn't even really a brother."

He had been. There was no denying that. Was that what had kept her from making her ogling more obvious? "Yeah, you were," she agreed. "Super annoying."

"I only did all of that to get your attention."

She tipped her head. "Why did you want my attention?"

"I don't think I really realized why. When I was doing it."

"Do you know now?"

He nodded. "Yeah, I think I do."

"Okay, why?" Her heart had sped up a little and she sat back, crossing her arms.

"Because when Riley Ames gives something, or someone, her attention, it means it's special. It's something she's given a lot of thought, and heart, to. It's really worthwhile."

Riley felt her mouth drop open.

"Like the music that you liked. You didn't just listen to the radio. You followed bands. You knew their backgrounds and their music that didn't get played regularly. You knew the meaning behind the lyrics. And the books you read. You didn't read whatever was most popular at the time. You found stories that really mattered to you. And your tattoos. You might have thought you were doing those to be rebellious, but every one of them has a meaning behind it."

Holy...crap.

"I guess I just wanted to be something that you gave some extra thought to. Even if it was annoyed thought."

"You didn't...you didn't feel worthwhile?"

He shrugged. "Not to you."

She shook her head. "I've always cared about you. You were

on my mind." She swallowed. "I think...I wanted to have a crush on you. But I wasn't your type."

He nodded. "I know. And ditto."

No, he hadn't been. She hadn't been. All of those things she'd been interested in—the books, the music, her hobbies— were nothing Derek had wanted to have anything to do with. But he'd been a teenage boy. He'd grown up a lot since then. He was a lot more mature and insightful than she'd ever given him credit for before.

She hadn't been his type before. He hadn't been her type before.

But now...

Those two words seemed to hang in the air, and Riley didn't dare say them. Or ask them.

"I didn't always like you," she acknowledged. "The idea of us being together never really occurred to me. But you always mattered."

He just looked at her for a long moment. "I was at the bookstore helping Lucy just now. She wants to have a stage built for Kade's book thing."

Riley wasn't sure why he was suddenly telling her this, but she nodded. "That was nice of you."

"You're not worried about that at all? That I wanted to date Lucy, and I went over first thing this morning to help her out?"

Riley frowned. "Of course not."

He paused another long moment. Then said simply, "I need a shower."

Her body instantly heated. It was the way he was looking at her. Or the idea of him naked and wet. Or the way he'd made her come already so many times. Or the way he'd held her. Or the fact that they had an imperfect history but still liked each other. Or all of the above. She nodded. "Me too."

With that, he pushed away from the counter, strode toward

her, tugged her to her feet, and lifted her over his shoulder. His big hand covered her ass as he carried her into the bathroom.

———

Three weeks.

Derek couldn't remember the last time he'd dated a woman for three weeks.

But he also couldn't remember a time when he'd had so much fun. Riley Ames was fun.

"Okay, I don't know what your love affair with onions is all about," Riley said, wiping her mouth with a napkin. "But you *have* to pull back."

It had taken him a week to actually get her to taste his pizza. She'd loved the barbecue chicken and the Everything Goes that he'd first introduced her to. Her favorite so far was the pepperoni and cream cheese, but she also really liked the taco pizza. Tonight, he'd pulled out a couple more specialty pizzas. The Philly cheesesteak, apparently, had too many onions.

"Fine." He jotted down a note.

"And I think you need a different seasoning on the beef. This almost tastes like fajita meat."

Their eyes met and they both smiled and said "fajita pizza" at the same time.

Riley laughed. "That might work. But cool it with the onions."

"Yes, I've *got it*." He reached over and snagged one of the onions, popping it in his mouth. "I think you're wrong, but I'll pull back."

She nodded and hopped down from where she'd been perched on the countertop. "As long as you do whatever I tell you, you're going to be fine."

He watched her ass as she headed for the fridge and a bottle of water.

"As long as the only thing you boss me about is the pizza, I'm going to be fine," he said.

She turned to face him, twisting the top of the bottle off. "Is that right?"

"It is." He leaned back, folding his arms. "You put too many chocolate chips in the chocolate chip pancakes, and you put too much orange juice in screwdrivers."

Riley came back toward him. "First, there's no such thing as too many chocolate chips in anything."

"It's like having a pile of chocolate chips with a little pancake batter around them."

She stopped in front of him, tipping her head back. She smiled. "Exactly. Perfect."

When she was close enough to touch, he couldn't keep his hands to himself. He lifted a finger and dragged it along the neckline of her off-the-shoulder tee. "And while sweet is perfectly fine when screwing, you also have to have the *drive* to make it really good."

She laughed. "The vodka is the *drive*?"

"Yep. The drive has to be there with the sweet."

She stepped even closer and ran her hand up his chest. "I gotta admit that you have a point there. I'll concede."

"I love when you concede."

"I know you do."

He bent and she lifted onto tiptoe, their lips almost touching, when the kitchen door swung open.

"Hey, need an extra hand up here."

Derek gave a little growl. But he was at work. "Yeah, okay," he told Bryan. "I'll be right there."

Riley settled back onto her feet with a little giggle. She lifted her water bottle for a drink. Derek just watched her. They'd had a lot of sex. A lot. And he still wanted her. All the time.

He hadn't slept with a woman this much in...ever. His relationships simply didn't span *weeks*, and even if they were more than a one-weekend thing, he certainly didn't see them, and have them spending the night, every single night.

Riley had practically moved in.

Her schedule was nearly as erratic as his. He'd get called for odd jobs here and there. She'd get called to help Scott and his task force out with things at any hour. She was sometimes at his kitchen table working when he came in for a shower or a sandwich during the day. She was sometimes propped up on his couch when he came in at night. And sometimes she wasn't. Sometimes she was at the station until past closing time at the Come Again. But then there were the nights when they were both at the Come Again, him behind the bar and her at her usual table, working. They'd make eye contact across the room, share little smiles, flirt when she came up for a coffee or water refill. And, of course, there were the times he'd pull her into the kitchen or back room for a quick make-out session just because he couldn't stand not kissing her for another minute.

All in all, things were really good. Comfortable. Happy.

Which was freaking him out a little.

Riley wasn't a traditional girl. She didn't do things the way other people did. It seemed in character that she'd accidentally start dating someone that she'd been coaching in how to be a good boyfriend to someone else. But falling for that guy and making it a long-term thing did *not* seem like her MO. Especially if that guy was pretty rooted in Sapphire Falls and had been a regular at her mom's dinner table even before they'd started seeing each other.

Yeah, it felt like they were dating, for sure. But it also kind of felt like they were two people who had known each other for a long time and had become friends over the past few weeks and were just hanging out. Banging each other on a regular basis too, of course, but also just hanging out.

Friends with benefits. That was exactly what this felt like.

Except for the fact that Derek was pretty sure he was in love with her.

He did know Riley well enough to know that telling her that was probably a really good way to end it all. And he didn't want to end it. Not the sex. But also not the advice they were giving each other about their jobs, and the support he was lending with her family and just the fun they had.

The whole thing would feel far too cliché for Riley. So it was better to just keep his mouth shut. Especially when he felt the urge to say, "I love you".

"Guess I'd better get to work." He pushed away from the counter.

She nodded. "Guess so." She picked up a piece of the pizza and took a bite.

"More? Really?" he asked. "I thought you said it has too many onions and not the right seasoning."

She nodded. "I did say that. Fewer onions and another seasoning would make this amazing. But it's pretty good anyway." She took another bite.

Derek shook his head but laughed. "I guess I did want you to be honest."

She swallowed and smiled. "I'll always be that."

He started toward the front of the bar but he hesitated, turned back, pulled her in and kissed her forehead. "Thank you." It was not sexy or flirtatious, but it felt right.

Her eyes were soft when he pulled back and looked down.

"You're welcome."

Then he got to work.

But an hour later, things were slow. Two bartenders was one too many. Finally, Bryan said, "Why don't you go hang out with your girl for a while?" He nodded toward Riley.

Derek took a deep breath. Was she his girl?

The vibe in the bar at ten p.m. was more laid-back and fun than it was after midnight, when the after-hours crowd came in to work and study. Now, even Riley was sitting with a soda and laughing and talking to Lucy and Peyton and a couple of other local girls.

Derek took a second to study the group. Peyton was hard not to notice. She was bright and loud and funny. She was a little more easygoing now that she was with Scott and felt more settled, but she was still outspoken and impossible to ignore. Samantha was another of the girls. She was the only one in the group who was married. She had a baby boy at home, but her friend, Kendall, also sitting with the group, made sure Samantha got out once in a while for a girls' night. And then there were Riley and Lucy.

They seemed completely different on the outside. Lucy wore very little makeup, generally kept her hair pulled back in a ponytail. She wore, well, basic clothes. Nothing in wild colors or particularly fitted or short. She smiled easily but was quiet and unassuming.

Riley was...none of those things. She was a lot like Peyton in that she was very hard to ignore, and Derek knew he wasn't the only man to feel that way. Her red hair, her dramatic makeup, her tattoos and bright-colored clothing were part of it. But her smile was big, her laugh was big, and she could be ready to argue nearly anything with anyone in a snap. Unassuming was *not* a word that would ever be assigned to Riley.

How could he think about dating Lucy? She was so nice. Smart. Sweet. He knew there was a man out there who would appreciate and love Lucy exactly as she was, but for *him*, well, he wasn't sure he could do quiet, nice, and sweet now.

Peyton had pulled Kendall and Samantha out onto the dance floor, and Riley and Lucy were sitting, just watching. He saw Dawson Hayes heading in their direction, and Derek fought the urge to step in front of the guy and tell him to back off, because he knew that Hayes was beelining for Riley.

Derek and Riley had been keeping their relationship on the

down low. No one knew they were seeing each other. No one knew that she was his.

His.

Derek frowned. That seemed damned possessive. Like the night a few weeks ago when Scott had first called her in to work and Derek had actually worried about her. And missed her.

He didn't do these things with women. But watching Dawson ask Riley to dance, and her accept, made Derek very much want to claim her. Loudly. Publicly.

And once he did that, he couldn't very well take it back. Riley was Kyle's little sister. Erika and Jake's daughter. Ruby's granddaughter. Once he said she was his, he wouldn't be able to take it back.

He still wanted to say it.

He started around the end of the bar, determined to cut in. In a very grand-gesture kind of way. But Riley looked up at him when he was only halfway across the floor. She tipped her head in the direction of the table where Lucy sat, now alone. He followed her gaze. Lucy didn't look unhappy. She looked... resigned. And yeah, okay, that made him feel a little like asking her to dance.

He glanced back at Riley. She widened her eyes and then nodded toward Lucy again.

Derek sighed. Yeah, yeah, he was going to ask Lucy to dance.

And, not for the first time, he wished that Riley was a little clingier. Why couldn't Dawson dance with Lucy? Why didn't Riley suggest that? *She* had a boyfriend. Lucy didn't.

But he turned, walked over to Lucy, held out a hand, said something charming, got a smile, and pulled the quiet bookworm onto the dance floor. And was rewarded with a big grin from the woman he was seriously considering spanking later.

And five hours later, after they'd danced and laughed, after he'd made sure Lucy had a fabulous time, after he'd leaned in and told Riley that he expected her mouth around his cock two minutes after they got home, after everyone had finally vacated the bar, they'd headed out to his truck hand in hand. And Derek admitted that he liked that Riley knew she could trust him, that he could dance with other women without her needing to worry. He liked that he didn't have to report in to her on a regular basis, that they could each do their own things and then end up back together at home.

But he still spanked her, because she asked very nicely.

Riley tore open the bag of sparkly sapphire-blue stones with a swarm of butterflies in her stomach. They were perfect. Beautiful and bright. They were going to look amazing scattered among the white and silver stones.

"Oh, those are so pretty!"

She looked up and smiled at Lucy. "They are, aren't they?"

Lucy was helping her get the path finished before the big crowd came to town for Michael Kade's murder-mystery event.

"Okay, so the white and silver stones are to fill up the path," Lucy clarified.

Thanks to Derek, the path was already dug. It curved from the highway on the edge of town, through the grass and trees that bordered the town, to Teal Street, the first street in Sapphire Falls. The path then continued through the town square from Teal Street to the gazebo that was the heart of the town. The path signified that anyone was welcome in Sapphire Falls and would find safety and hospitality. It was also designed to raise awareness among the people in Sapphire Falls and their visitors for victims of sex trafficking that were often taken from their own homes to places far away, where they were alone and scared.

The square saw the most traffic of anywhere in town, and

when the people of Sapphire Falls walked by the path, or even followed the path up to the gazebo, they'd think of what it stood for. And when visitors saw the unusual path, made of loose white, silver, and blue stones, and they asked what it was about, anyone in town should be able to tell them.

"Yes, those are just the basic fillers," Riley said. "And then every person or family or business who donates five dollars gets a blue stone to add to the path. Hopefully, some families and all the businesses will donate more than one stone."

All the money would go to an advocacy group called the Family Alliance. Her parents had actually given her the money to create the path and buy the stones, so that all the proceeds could be donated. She still got a little choked up when she thought about that.

"I love it," Lucy told her. "It's beautiful, and I love the symbolism."

Riley smiled. "Thanks, Luce." She was really proud of it. And she loved that Derek had helped her build it, and that her mom and dad had given her the money to get it started, and that Lucy was here helping her now.

"And you're doing the official ceremony where everyone adds their stones the morning of the event?"

"Yes. I figure people will be sure to be in town because of the event, and we'll have lots of visitors too. Everyone can gather here, put their stones in, and then head to the event."

"Wonderful," Lucy said. She bit her bottom lip, then said, "I have an idea to add, if you want to hear it."

"Of course." Riley set the bag of stones down. "What are you thinking?"

"So we have the path here, and you're going to do a little speech explaining everything at the gazebo."

"Right."

"Then what if we have a path that leads from here over to the bookstore? We're going to start the murder mystery there.

We could set up tables a few yards apart between here and there. Some of the tables could have educational materials, a few could have refreshments, a couple could maybe have people from the task force or from Family Alliance to answer questions or give people even more information."

Riley was staring at her. "Lucy, that's a fabulous idea!"

"You think so?" Lucy gave her a small smile.

Riley stepped over the bag of rocks and gathered her friend in for a hug. "I do. I think that's great." She stepped back, holding Lucy's upper arms. "Are you sure though? That day is also about Kade and the event too."

"Of course. The whole idea of the event is to show people around the town he based Aquamarine Ridge on. We'll have people walking all over town and they'll definitely see this. It will educate them too. Maybe they'll even go back to their communities and see what they can do. And," Lucy said with a shrug, "it was actually Hannah's idea."

"Oh." Riley nodded. "That makes sense." Hannah was Michael Kade's best friend, and the reason he'd ended up in Sapphire Falls in the first place. It was a well-known fact that she hated that Kade had set a gruesome murder mystery in a town that resembled her sweet, beloved hometown *very* closely.

Lucy nodded. "She says this will show people how *nice* Sapphire Falls really is. Apparently, there are some internet rumors that Kade's book is actually based on a true story."

Riley laughed. Then she focused on Lucy. "Wait, it isn't, is it?" Lucy knew everything about Sapphire Falls' history. If there was a bloody unsolved murder in the town's past, she'd know it. Riley frowned. She hadn't read the book, but Derek had. He was a huge fan and had the book on the coffee table at his house. She'd flipped through it one night, reading bits and pieces. "But there are vampires in Kade's book, right?"

"Well, there are *suspicions* of vampires in Kade's book."

"So, I mean, *that* couldn't have happened. The internet rumor is just about the murder then?"

Lucy shook her head. "I didn't say that."

"The internet rumor is about there being *vampires* here too?"

"What I meant was, I didn't say that vampires couldn't have lived here," Lucy said.

Riley felt her eyes widen. "Excuse me?"

Lucy had always been into the macabre. She *loved* mysteries and ghost stories and murder and mayhem. But Riley had always kind of assumed that all of that was in Lucy's fictional world. She did study history, especially that of their little town, but Riley didn't think Lucy actually thought there were ghosts and things *in* Sapphire Falls for real.

"And there are definitely some suspicious deaths in Sapphire Falls' history," Lucy said. "This town isn't all sunshine and daisies, you know."

Huh. Riley thought that about 98% of the town would actually argue that with Lucy. "So you helped Kade with his research?"

"I might have pushed a couple of file folders under his door at the boarding house," Lucy said. Then she gave Riley a proud grin.

Riley laughed. "Oh my gosh, you're so funny. I suppose you've arranged some kind of ghost tour of the town?"

Lucy's eyes brightened as she nodded and Riley groaned, but was still smiling. "That's hilarious."

"And Derek has agreed to take people through the cemetery and give some history there too."

At the mention of his name, Riley's heart gave a little stutter. Then she frowned. Derek hadn't mentioned that he was doing any tours for the book event. He'd only told her that he was helping with things at the bookshop, like building the stage and helping Lucy with some of the bigger cleaning jobs. She'd needed to make more room in the shop and had been moving bookshelves and things around. She'd kept Derek busy hauling books out of the lower level of the shop to the second floor, where Lucy lived over the store.

Riley shook her head. It didn't matter that he hadn't mentioned it. He loved these books and had been excited about the event since it had first been announced. She was glad he was going to get to help and have fun with it.

"He's been so helpful," Lucy went on. "I really don't know how I would have done this without him." She smiled. "He's really sweet. And funny."

He was. Or could be, anyway. Riley nodded and picked up a bag of white rocks to fill the path, suddenly wanting to be busy for some reason.

"I know you were worried that he might try to, I don't know…"

Riley looked up. "He might try to what?"

Lucy shook her head. She almost looked embarrassed. "That he might flirt or something," she said.

Riley was shocked to feel a surge of relief. *He's not flirting because he's very happy at home.* She smiled. They hadn't told anyone they were seeing each other. They hadn't really told *each other* that they were seeing each other. But she didn't know what else to call it. They saw each other every day, told each other what they were up to—okay, with the exception of Derek not telling her about the cemetery tours—and they spent almost every night together. That was, pretty much, dating. She supposed. Kind of. Even if it was a big secret. But maybe it was time to tell someone.

Riley opened her mouth to reply to Lucy, but before she could, Lucy said, "But it's all been very sweet. Very appropriate. Romantic. He doesn't treat me like the girls I've seen him flirting with at the Come Again. He's a lot more respectful."

A chill swept over her, and Riley realized she was having a

hard time taking a deep breath. "He's been...romantic?" she asked, trying her best to sound normal. "How so?"

"He brought me coffee the last couple of mornings," Lucy said.

"Oh, that's nice," Riley agreed. "But romantic?"

"He put caramel creamer in it," Lucy said with a smile. "He said he remembered that's how I've ordered it at the Come Again before. And," her smile grew, "he added extra whipped cream. Remember that night when we had hot chocolate and you didn't want any but he put the extra on mine?"

Oh, yeah, she remembered that. "I do."

"And he brought scones with the coffee yesterday."

Scones? *Scones?* It was one thing to put some extra coffee in one of his to-go cups and take it along when he left the house. He already had the stupid creamer tubs all over his kitchen. But scones meant he'd made an extra stop.

"And while we worked, he put music on his phone," Lucy said.

Riley nodded. He often had it on in the kitchen at the bar and at home when he was cleaning or doing yard work. "He likes to work to music." She honestly didn't care at this point if Lucy wondered how Riley would know that.

"But it was Lindsey Stirling."

Okay, Lindsey Stirling was pretty amazing, but not only could Riley not imagine Derek listening to violin music while he worked—even really cool violin music—but she'd never heard him listen to it around the house or at the Come Again. While Lucy loved Lindsey Stirling. "How did he know you like her?" she asked.

"He's heard it in the bookstore," Lucy said. "I had unplugged the stereo and taken it upstairs, so I didn't have any music on, but he'd heard it before. He said we couldn't plan a kick-ass book event without inspiration, so he pulled it up on his phone. I wouldn't have minded listening to something else, but it was sweet of him."

It really was. Riley frowned and dumped her bag of rocks out, thinking. Seemed that Derek had made a lot of notes about Lucy and the things she liked. He'd obviously spent enough time in the bookstore to know these details. And making a woman coffee with her favorite creamer was hardly a stretch for him.

"So I wanted to ask you something," Lucy said.

Oh, God, she was going to ask Riley if she'd be okay with Lucy dating Derek. And Lucy didn't even know that Riley and Derek were sleeping together. She just thought that Riley thought he was an idiot who didn't know how to treat a nice girl.

And clearly Derek had proven *that* wrong over the past several days with Lucy.

Riley grabbed another bag, ripped it open and dumped the stones onto the dirt path. That Derek had dug for her in between all the cleaning and hauling and stage-building he'd been doing for Lucy. When he wasn't getting her scones and playing her favorite music.

"Riley, are you okay?"

She stopped and looked up at Lucy. Sweet, beautiful, staying-in-Sapphire-Falls-forever, deserves-a-guy-who-makes-her-coffee Lucy. "Yeah, I'm fine. Why?"

"You just went to work, ripping through those bags like you were suddenly possessed."

Possessed. Yeah, she felt a little possessed. Or *possessive*. As in, she was feeling possessive. Of Derek.

She dropped the bag she was holding and stared at Lucy.

Dammit. How had that happened? She was supposed to be making Derek good boyfriend material *for someone else*. Or scaring him off entirely. Either way, she'd failed. Miserably.

Because he was already good boyfriend material. And he didn't seem scared off, at all. And she wanted to keep him.

"Riley? Are you *sure* you're feeling okay?" Lucy asked, clearly concerned.

Nope. She really wasn't. She had to confess to Lucy that she was a bad friend and had slept with—and fallen in love with—the guy she'd been trying to turn into a good guy for *someone else*. Like Lucy. "I—"

She was saved from answering by someone calling her name. She turned to find Scott coming across the town square toward her. She wasn't sure if she felt relieved. Or like puking.

A little of both honestly.

"Hey, Scott." Okay, that was too bright. She shouldn't be that happy to see Scott.

"Hey, Riley. Hi, Lucy."

"Hi, Scott."

Scott was the town cop but he never went by "Officer". Unless it was with Peyton. And she called him that in a flirty, hot way that made everyone around them very clear about how he used his handcuffs at home.

He looked at the path. "How's it coming?"

"Great," Riley told him, giving a no-big-deal-everything-is-fine shrug. "It will definitely be ready in time."

She made herself focus on the path. She was proud of it. Not everything about being back in Sapphire Falls had gone according to plan. Like the whole falling-in-love-with-Derek thing. The work with the task force and the advocacy efforts had been a surprising addition to her life as well, but it was all good.

"It looks great," Scott said.

The path was curved to signify that it wasn't always a straight shot to what you wanted, but the stones that would sparkle in the sunlight and under the lights that lit the square at night were a symbol that there was beauty and light even on those curvy paths.

It was going to be awesome. And, yes, she loved that she was seeing her idea come to life and that Derek had been a part of it. He'd gone with her to talk to the mayor about digging up the square. He'd removed the grass and helped her prepare the path for the stones. He hadn't been able to help with the stones or the sign, but she knew he loved the project.

"So, hey, I have something to ask you about," Scott said.

She took a deep breath and lifted a hand to shield her eyes from the sun. "Okay."

"I think you should consider the police academy."

If he'd told her that he'd stolen a unicorn and needed her to hide it for him, she wouldn't have been more surprised. Or confused. "*What*?"

Scott was in uniform, and his badge winked at her in the sunlight as he shifted and propped his hands on his hips. "Sorry, I don't have time to ease into it and you're a pretty straightforward girl," he said. "I think you should think about the police academy. Becoming a police officer. Then you should come back here and work with me. Ed is going to be retiring and I need someone. You have a really special skill set that has, obviously, been crucial to getting some big stuff done. We would absolutely have you continue working with the task force. But you could do even more. And I've watched you. I think you've really enjoyed the work, you've enjoyed doing something big and important and helping people, and I think you'd be great at it."

"Wow, Scott, I don't know what to say." She really didn't. But he was right about everything—she did love the work.

"Just think about it, okay?" he asked. "We can talk more later."

"Okay. I will." She'd probably not be able to avoid it anyway.

She watched Scott walk away. Wow. A job. One that she could really care about. Where she could use what she was good at and do something that mattered.

"Oh my God, Riley!" Lucy exclaimed.

Riley had almost forgotten she was there. In an uncharacteristic display of enthusiasm, Lucy grabbed her in a hug. "You might stay?" she asked. She pulled back. "Really? You might live here in Sapphire Falls?"

Riley processed that. Yeah, being a cop in Sapphire Falls would mean living here in Sapphire Falls. Long term. Maybe even forever.

A weird sense of panic gripped her chest, and she struggled to take a deep breath. "Oh, geez, I don't know," she said, forcing a smile and wondering if Lucy could hear the shakiness in her voice. "I mean, that would be pretty huge."

"It would," Lucy agreed, still more enthusiastic than Riley had seen her get about anything in a long time. "But hey, just because it's huge doesn't mean it's *bad*. I'd love to have you here! Oh wow," Lucy gushed, her smile big and bright. "I can't believe it. I might have my best friend move back to town. I have *Michael Kade* living here and doing a book event at my store. I might be *dating someone*." She took a deep breath. "This is all so amazing. And huge." She gave Riley a grin. "See? Huge doesn't mean bad."

Dating someone. That was all Riley really heard.

Lucy was thinking about dating Derek.

And why wouldn't she be? He was being sweet to her. It wasn't flirting like he usually did, but then he'd been learning about what it was like to romance a nice girl. And he'd had a *very* good teacher.

And of course Derek was thinking of dating Lucy. That's how this had all started. *He* didn't know that Riley had been messing around when she'd been "teaching" him to be a nice-girl boyfriend.

"Hey, Lucy, has Derek mentioned you guys having lunch again or anything?"

Lucy shook her head. "No. Why?"

So, he was being sweet, even romantic, but he hadn't actually asked her out. Yet.

At least, he was a nice enough guy to wait for things with Riley to end.

Because they would. Of course. Because she would leave, eventually. Supposedly. It had never been a secret that she had no plans to stay in Sapphire Falls.

Would he be shocked that Scott had offered her a job? A job that she could admit she would really like. And be good at.

But maybe that wouldn't really matter. Even if she stayed, it wasn't like Derek would be counting on things between them lasting. Neither of them were really known for long-term relationships. They were basically friends who were having sex. Really good sex, but still. They'd always been in each other's lives. That wouldn't change. Their families were friends, they had history, her brother was his best friend. The sex part couldn't keep up though.

People who were good friends and then had sex...forever... were, well...married.

And she and Derek were *not* going to get married.

Her stomach knotted suddenly and she felt sick. "Um, I, um...I think I need to go," she said. She looked around. Where was she going to go?

"So you're *not* feeling well," Lucy said. "I could tell."

"Yeah, I'm definitely not feeling well."

And for the first time in a very long time, years in fact, she felt like going home, curling up on the couch, and letting her mom fuss over her.

11

The fussing was going to have to wait.

Riley had managed to get curled up on the couch, but Erika wasn't available for fussing. She was busy getting the house ready for the dinner party they were having that night. That included Kyle and Hannah, their grandmother, and, for some reason, Derek. And his parents.

Okay, Derek being there wasn't a big surprise. He'd eaten countless meals at her mother's dining room table over the years and had been over a couple of times just in the past few weeks. They'd had to work on hiding their feelings or anything that might let on that they were more than...what they'd always been.

But were they? That was what was bothering her. She and Derek *were* the same they'd always been. She still felt she could be completely honest with him and that he was completely honest with her. She could tell him when she hated his shirt, or that dipping his French fries in mayo was disgusting. But she could also now tell him that she liked his haircut and that he made amazing pizza, and that she just flat out liked *him* and that *he* was amazing. As kids and teens, she would have *never* admitted that she liked something about him, or that he was doing something right. Because, well, they'd been kids and teens, and that's how they interacted.

But now…

She pulled the throw pillow over her face, groaning.

He was amazing.

And she wanted to keep doing what they'd been doing. For a very long time.

Which had to be the most cliché, sickening thing she'd ever done.

She'd gotten out. She'd gone away. She'd had a great job and apartment in California.

And now she was back in Sapphire Falls, living with her parents, crushing on her brother's best friend—the biggest playboy in town, of course—and another of her brother's friends was creating a job for her.

Apparently orgasms made her brain mushy. And distracted her from the fact that she had fallen into the rut of Sapphire Falls.

"Riley? Can you help me with the table?" Erika called from the kitchen.

Riley tossed the pillow and sighed up at the ceiling. Of course she could. And should. Lying on the couch, *not* being fussed over wasn't helping. Though she doubted the fussing would really help anyway. This wasn't a poor-baby-chicken-soup problem. This was a shit-what-am-I-going-to-do problem.

Riley padded into the kitchen. "What can I do?"

Her mom looked over. Then frowned. "Are you going to change before dinner?"

Riley looked down at her capris and tank top. "Do I need to?"

"We're having people over."

"Yeah. *Our* people. People I've known forever. They've seen me dressed like this before." *And Derek doesn't seem to mind when I'm dressed down. Or not dressed at all.*

She stopped those thoughts immediately. That didn't matter, and she *definitely* needed to not think about being undressed with Derek while standing with her mother in the kitchen of her childhood home.

Then Erika shocked her by putting down the dish towel she held, leaning back against the counter behind her, and studying Riley.

That never happened when there was a meal to prepare. And there was always a meal to prepare.

It struck Riley that maybe there was something there. Derek had said he'd given her a hard time and teased her because he'd wanted her attention. Had that been part of why Riley acted out and did the opposite of everything Kyle did? To get her mom's attention? Even if it wasn't the most positive way to do that?

"Our people," Erika repeated. "I like that."

Riley nodded, suddenly feeling nervous.

"Do you really feel that way?"

Riley wet her lips. "Of course."

"They're not just *my* people? They're *our* people?" Erika pressed.

"Yes. Of course. Kyle and Hannah are definitely *our* people."

"And the Wrights?" Erika asked.

"They've been like a part of the family for as long as I can remember," Riley replied honestly. There had always been barbecues and game nights and holiday parties shared with the Wrights.

"And Derek?"

Oh boy. There it was. She shrugged. "Derek too. He's always been like another big brother. I can hardly think of a time when he wasn't around. He's definitely seen me looking way worse than this."

She really hoped like hell she wasn't blushing.

Erika nodded. "I suppose that's true." She paused, then said, "Longtime friendships like that can be complicated. We sometimes take them for granted. Or think that things will always be the same no matter what, so we don't watch what we do and say as carefully as we do with other people."

It had been a long time since Erika and Riley had had a heart-to-heart. A really long time. Riley shifted her weight. "Are you talking in general or about something specific?" she asked.

"You and Derek have been spending a lot of time together."

Riley nodded. "And you don't like that?"

Erika frowned. "I didn't say that. You always assume that what I'm saying is a criticism."

"It often is."

"Because you're often pushing my buttons."

Riley took a deep breath, then acknowledged that with a nod. "Sometimes." She sighed. "I don't know why I do that."

Erika lifted a shoulder. "I don't know why I criticize." She paused. "Well, maybe I do."

Riley tipped her head. "Why?"

"It started off that I was worried," Erika told her. "I knew how to handle a kid like Kyle. I knew what to expect. Then you came along and did everything differently and I didn't know how it would turn out. Then...I guess it was a way to feel like you still needed me. To get your attention."

Surprise rocked through Riley. "*You* were trying to get *my* attention?"

"You never really needed anyone, Riley. You didn't ask me for advice on your clothes or how to handle your friends or teachers. You didn't even ask me about your period."

Riley opened her mouth, then shut it again. Her mom was right. She hadn't gone to Erika for much, because she'd assumed her mother's advice would have been to do it like Kyle did it, or to at least do the opposite of whatever Riley was doing.

"I guess I was trying to insert myself into your life when you didn't ask me in," Erika said. "And it often came out as criticism." She sighed like Riley had. "It took me a while to admit that you were doing fine on your own. And that annoyed me."

Riley felt herself smile. "I didn't *always* do fine."

"You always ended up fine in the end."

She scoffed at that. "Really? Fine? I'm back here in Sapphire Falls, living with you guys, jobless except for what my brother's friend gives me to do."

"I thought you liked the job with Scott."

She felt her heart trip slightly. "I do. I love it actually."

"Then does it matter how you got it? It's still about your talent and skills."

Riley looked at her mom. She thought Riley had talent and skills. "It just feels like I should be able to make some things happen for myself. Things here are...easy. I guess that's nice," she added quickly. "But it's maybe a little less satisfying when things just...happen, rather than me making them happen."

"Are things with Derek easy?"

The air seemed to rush out of her lungs. Her mom was asking specifically about Derek. Oh boy. "Wha—what do you mean?"

"I mean your relationship with Derek," Erika said, giving her a look that made Riley certain her mom knew exactly what she and Derek had been up to. "Is it easy?"

Riley finally nodded. "Yeah. Really easy. In fact..." She thought about what she was about to admit, but realized that her and Derek's relationship, no matter what it was exactly, impacted their families. "It happened accidentally. He was thinking about dating Lucy, and I decided to give him some tips on how to be a better boyfriend and...things just happened.' She blew out a breath. "It was very easy."

Erika nodded slowly. "I would think that it would be."

"Really?" Her heart skipped for some reason.

"You've known each other a long time, you're a lot alike, you're very comfortable together."

Yep, all of that had contributed for sure. "But it feels...accidental," Riley said, lifting her shoulder. "It wasn't supposed to happen at all. So it's not like we're taking it very seriously."

Erika frowned. "That's what I was afraid of."

"What?"

"That you were just messing around."

Riley nodded. "Yeah. Pretty much." She ignored the voice in her head that was calling bullshit.

"Your brother seems to think that it's more than that," Erika said.

Riley's eyebrows shot up. "You and Kyle have talked about this?"

"Of course." Erika said it as if she and Kyle discussed Riley and her life choices all the time.

Which they probably did.

"He's thrilled."

Riley blinked at her. "What? Kyle is thrilled that Derek and I are messing around?"

"No. He's thrilled that you and Derek are *dating*," Erika said. "He loves the idea of you both settling down, and the fact that it's together is even better."

Well...*crap.*

"We're not settling down together," Riley said. "I'm not settling down at all." Her stomach ache was definitely back.

"Kyle said Scott offered you a more long-term job."

Of course Scott had told Kyle that, and Kyle had told her mother. "He did. But I didn't give him an answer."

"And Kyle thinks you and Derek are getting serious."

Riley took a breath. "Well, Kyle hasn't asked *me* about that." Then something occurred to her. She frowned. "Did *Kyle* ask Scott to make me that job offer?"

Erika shook her head. "I don't know. I don't think so." Then she frowned. "But would that be so bad? He's your big brother. He's just looking out for you. He wants you here. Why is that something bad?"

"Because I don't need his help."

"You don't have a job," Erika pointed out.

Riley tipped her head back with a soft "argh". Then she met her mother's eyes. "I haven't made good decisions 100% of the time, I'll admit. I've messed some things up. But I don't want or need the Sapphire Falls contingency plan put into place."

Erika propped a hand on her hip. "Don't you? Where else would you have gone after your jail time was over?"

Her accidental and forgiven jail time. At least forgiven by the courts. "Just because I temporarily needed a place to go doesn't mean that I've given up entirely."

"And that's what it would be if you came back for good, got a job here, started a serious relationship here?" Erika asked. "Giving up?"

Riley felt frustration and confusion building. Sapphire Falls was fine. It was great even. For some people. But being here really was easy. *Staying* here would be even easier. Following in her brother's footsteps and being like everyone else she knew here would be easy. At least until she started doing things like joining committees or, God forbid, having to *arrest* someone here, or for sure if she had kids here. She'd want to do things differently. She'd want to have a say. She'd want to make them think about things differently. And that wouldn't be welcomed.

"Yes, okay?" she finally answered her mother. "If I stay here, fall into the job that Scott offered, get involved with some guy whose greatest accomplishment is the first-place trophy from the demo derby last summer, then yeah, that's giving up."

There was a long, tense moment without either of them blinking.

Then Riley heard someone clear his throat behind her and

say, "Well, I *did* unseat the three-time champion to get that trophy."

Riley felt regret and a definite sense of "well fuck" go through her. She slowly turned to face Derek.

"I didn't know you were there." She hadn't been talking about him anyway. Probably. She knew about the trophy on the top of his bookcase, but she knew it wasn't his greatest accomplishment. Not by far.

"I just came in. Front door was open. Lucy said you weren't feeling well. I came over to check on you."

Yeah, she most definitely wasn't feeling well. As a matter of fact, the idea of caramel coffee creamer made her want to throw up at the moment. "You didn't have to do that. I know you and Lucy have a lot to get ready for the murder-mystery thing."

He nodded. "I didn't mind taking a break. Though I went to my house first. Thought maybe you'd be working over there."

Typically, she would have been. "After Lucy told me everything you guys had going on, I figured I wouldn't be seeing you much anyway. And Mom needed help with dinner."

Not that she'd known that when she'd come over, but it seemed like a better excuse to give him than, "I was feeling jealous and realizing that we've made a big mistake and decided to come over here and feel sorry for myself and try to avoid everything that reminds me of you, but of course I can't do that because everything here in Sapphire Falls seems to remind me of you."

"You'd be seeing me just like you always do, when I'm done with work," he said with a frown.

"I don't know, it just sounded like Lucy needed more of your time and attention."

Oh, God, *that* sounded jealous and bitchy.

He arched a brow, which told her clearly that he thought so too. "The event is coming up."

"And I know you're really invested in it," she said with a nod. "I hear you're doing cemetery tours for her."

"I wouldn't say they're *for her*," he said mildly. "They're for the readers."

"Well, whatever. I get that it's going to take a lot of your time. And it's not like you *have* to spend time with me." She glanced at her mom. "We're just hanging out."

He didn't look impressed. "I don't know. I'm concerned. Seems that you've come down with a bad case of bitch-itis."

Riley's eyes went wide, and she thought maybe she heard her mom snort.

But he wasn't wrong. She was being a brat to her mom. She'd also hurt his feelings, she was sure. She was having a bad day. Falling in love could do that to a girl. Apparently.

"But I can take care of it. Let's go." Derek reached for her arm but she shrugged back, making him miss.

"No."

He sighed. "We really need to talk."

"Look, I know you," she said. "I know you don't like the long-term girlfriend thing and the clingy, jealous bit. I get it. I've seen your mom and dad."

"Riley!" her mom exclaimed.

"Oh, come on," Riley said. "We all know it. We love her, but she's needy."

"Ril—"

"It's okay, Erika," Derek said. His eyes were on Riley when she looked back at him. "She's right. And yes, that's why I didn't want a girlfriend."

"And why we're *just* hanging out," Riley said.

"Because you're the same way?"

That blunt question came from her mother. And she was right.

Riley didn't cling to things—like her hometown or traditions or jobs or relationships. She shrugged, pretending that her stomach wasn't knotting as she did it. "Exactly."

"Okay. Come on."

This time she wasn't fast enough to avoid Derek grabbing her hand and starting toward the front door.

"Derek, I don't want to talk," Riley protested, trying to pull free.

"Then I'll talk." He sighed as she dug her heels in. He turned, bent, and lifted her up over his shoulder.

She blew out a breath. What was the point of fighting really? If they didn't talk now, he'd find her another time. Hell, he was supposed to be over for dinner right here later tonight.

He carried her out to the front porch before setting her down. He pulled the door firmly shut behind them.

———

This woman was a huge pain in his ass.

And he was in love with her.

And she was about to try to break up with him.

"What the hell are you doing?" he asked.

"Me? You're the one manhandling me." Riley brushed her hands down the front of her shirt, pretending to be offended.

"Uh-huh." He crossed his arms and looked down at her.

She sighed. "Fine. I'm annoying my mom. You should recognize it—it happens a lot."

"Why were you and your mom talking about you giving up and staying here?"

She crossed her arms too. But she didn't look intimidating. She looked vulnerable. "Because Kyle got Scott to offer me a job."

"And?"

There was more to it than that. There had been that little show of jealousy he'd seen. He couldn't believe she actually thought he could possibly be interested in anyone else, but it *was* nice for someone who didn't stick to much to want to, at least subconsciously, stick to him. He didn't like clingy women. But he liked kind of clingy Riley. At least when she was clinging to *him*.

Riley lifted her chin. "And apparently Kyle is thrilled that we're settling down together. And Mom and I can't agree on what to name our twins."

He couldn't help it. He grinned. "Kyle knows?"

She rolled her eyes. "You didn't tell him?"

"We haven't talked about you."

"Why not?"

"Because there's nothing to talk about." He shrugged as he realized it. "We make sense. It seems natural."

She narrowed her eyes. "Easy."

"Yeah. It is easy. You agree."

"I do. It's been very easy hanging out with you and fucking you."

He knew that she was trying to piss him off. But that comment worked a little, he had to admit.

"So how about we just keep doing it?"

"No."

She said it very firmly. Far more firmly than was really necessary. "Why not?"

"Sapphire Falls is sucking me in. And the orgasms have been distracting me. I have to stop so I don't just keep saying yes to everything."

"Saying yes isn't so bad." He lifted a hand and fingered the end of the strand of hair lying against her shoulder.

She tipped her head. "Really?"

"What?"

"You want to keep tricking me into this rut."

His hand dropped. "This *rut*?"

"The easy way out."

Now he leaned back. "Excuse me?"

She blew out a breath. "Come on. You know what I'm talking about. People grow up here, they don't have any other options, so they just go along. They hook up with someone local, they take a job that's easy. Something their family or friends arrange. And they stay."

He nodded, his chest feeling tight. "Yep. That's what a lot of us do."

She shook her head. "I didn't mean *you*."

"Yes, you did. Everything you described is me. I grew up here. I took a job that was easy. I'm looking for someone local to hook up with."

"But this is what you *want*. That's different than just doing it because—"

"Because we don't have any other ambitions?"

She frowned. "I didn't say that."

"But that's what you see. You see that everything I've got just fell into my lap. Because I've just been sitting around here, my lap wide open."

And the thing was—that wasn't inaccurate.

Derek had never really had to work very hard for anything. This wasn't the first time it had occurred to him. It also wasn't the first time it had occurred to him that it made it hard for Riley to respect him. Did she like his business ideas? Yes. Did she think he was a hard worker? Yes. Did she believe and respect that he was happy? Sure. But he couldn't shake the idea that she thought he could do more if he tried harder.

"I'm not going to lie to you," she said.

He braced himself even as he felt a wave of relief. One thing he could count on was that he'd always know what was going on with Riley. He didn't have to guess with her. "Good."

"You've had a pretty easy life, Derek," she said. "Your biggest worry is if your pizza is good. And...it is. So, yeah, things are pretty sunny for you."

He knew he should be offended. And he was, a little. It wasn't like his life was perfect. But then again, she had a point.

"Are you so sure the hard way is the best way?" he asked.

She shrugged. "I've always liked doing things *my* way."

"And alone," he said.

Again her chin came up. "Yeah, well, I guess I don't need as much help as Lucy does. For instance."

He shook his head. "This isn't about Lucy."

"Isn't it? You're the most...helpful guy in this town. It would probably drive you crazy to be with someone who never needs you."

He sighed. That's what she was telling herself? That she didn't need him? Yeah, that would bother him. Yes, he loved being there for the people he cared about. But he knew that he needed a woman who could be okay with him being there for everyone else.

And Riley fucking needed him. For pep talks, to help buffer things with her mom. For orgasms.

That was no small thing.

Dammit.

"And I think that when Lucy asks you out, you should say yes."

He felt his scowl form immediately. "*What*?"

"I'm going to tell Lucy to ask you out."

He scrubbed a hand over his face. Pain. In. His. Ass. "Again, *what*?"

"Lucy thinks you're really sweet, and loved the scones and the Lindsey Stirling, and now she thinks you're ready to be a boyfriend. And you know what?" she added quickly. "I think she's right. You're definitely ready. In fact," she took a deep breath, "you've *been* ready. You haven't needed any training." She gave him a quick, bright smile. "So I guess we're done."

"We're *done*," Derek repeated. "Is that right?"

She nodded, but he saw her swallow hard. "I mean, we'll

still see each other and stuff. Like dinner tonight." She gave a laugh that was tight and completely fake. "But that was the main reason I was always at your house and around, so...no more early-morning walks or anything."

He watched her trying to talk herself into this bullshit, feeling his gut knotting.

But there was something that Riley was forgetting. He knew her.

"Okay, Riley, you win," he finally said.

She blinked at him. "I do?"

"You think I've always had it easy. Well, okay. I'm ready to do things the hard way."

"I don't know what you mean."

"You," he told her simply. "You're the hard thing I have to work at. And I'm ready."

As he said it to her, he realized that all sounded really good actually. If he worried that things came too easily for him, the universe had just presented him with a huge challenge in convincing Riley Ames she was in love with him.

She was already shaking her head as a matter of fact. "That's not what I meant."

He nodded. "Yeah, this is going to be good for both of us. I need to work at something, and you," he lifted a hand to her cheek, "you need someone who doesn't want you to be different at all." He leaned in and said by her ear, "You go right ahead and be a brat. I'm up for it." Then he kissed her temple and stepped back.

She looked like she wanted to cry. And like she wanted to launch herself into his arms. He grinned. "This is usually the part where you argue with me just to argue."

"You could really regret this," she said. But her voice lacked conviction.

Instead of arguing, he just smiled. "There's my girl." Then he turned and headed for his truck.

"See you at dinner?" she called after him.

Feeling triumphant, he looked back. "Nah. Tell your mom I can't make it."

Riley was clearly surprised. "Why not?"

"Stuff to do." He pulled the truck door open. "And I want to make you miss me a little bit."

She sighed. "You're a pain." But she didn't deny that she would maybe, possibly, miss him. A little.

"I love you too, Ry." Derek got in his truck with that and drove off.

Yes, he'd just told Riley he loved her. And as a bonus, she was now going to stew about it. How he'd done it, if he'd meant it, and how she felt about him.

He was humming as he pulled into the Come Again parking lot.

Yes, his life was pretty easy. But he loved it, and he couldn't wait to show Riley that things didn't have to be difficult to be satisfying.

12

———

She really hated when Derek was right. And when he proved that he knew her very well. She knew that *he* knew that she was stewing. That night all through dinner, and then in her room later because she refused to go to the Come Again or his house. If the guy was going to start dating someone seriously—someone who wasn't Riley—Riley had to not be around. Because she'd distract him. Not because seeing him with someone else would bother her. Because that was stupid. How could that bother her? She could have him if she wanted him. Apparently.

And *that* was why she was stewing. And she knew that he knew it.

He wanted her. He was going to work for her—whatever that meant. And he'd said he loved her. Kind of. It had sounded casual, like a flippant thing to say to a friend. But he'd never said it before. In all the time they'd spent together, he'd never said "love you" even flippantly. And there had been something in his eyes when he'd said it. Something that made her think... not flippant.

So, she avoided him for three days.

Three days that made her miss him and wonder about him and *want* him. Yes, she missed the sex—he was really, really good at that—but it was more.

And she really hated when he was right.

Riley heard a knock on her bedroom door. She sighed. She was getting nothing done anyway. She'd already read the entire police academy website. Four times.

"Yeah?" she called.

Her brother poked his head in a moment later. "Hey. Can I come in?"

"Sure." Riley shut her laptop and set it aside, crossing her legs on top of her comforter. "What's up?"

Kyle came through the door with something wrapped in white paper. "Got something for you."

She reached for it. "What is it?" It was wrapped like a bouquet of flowers but no blooms peeked out.

"From Derek."

Her eyes flew to her brother's. "What?"

Kyle nodded. "And I'm supposed to tell you that it's okay with me if you date him."

"I wasn't worried about that," Riley told him honestly.

"Good. That's what I told Derek."

"Actually, I'm more concerned you'll arrange our marriage."

Kyle tucked his hands into his pockets. "Yeah, I'm kind of a dick."

She snorted.

But Kyle's smile faded. "Look, Riley, here's the deal—"

"I know. I make bad decisions and you think I need your help."

He shook his head. "I'm not *worried* about you. Derek isn't some kind of solution for making you more responsible or something."

She crossed her arms. "Then what's he a solution for?"

"For making you happy."

The air whooshed from her lungs. "You don't just want me with him so I stay here forever and settle down and quit going to jail?"

Kyle gave a little laugh. "You should quit going to jail no matter where you live, Ry."

Okay, he had a point. "It's just all too…"

"Easy," he filled in when she trailed off. "Derek told me."

She frowned. "You can't see at all what I mean? That I'm just falling into all of this? Taking the easy way out?"

Kyle blew out a breath and sat on the edge of her desk. "Riley, it's not supposed to be hard. They don't call it *digging* into love. It's not *climbing* into love. It's not *pushing* or fighting into love. They call it *falling* into love. Falling is easy. You just let yourself go and it happens."

Her throat felt tight. "You and Hannah had to work at it," she pointed out.

But he shook his head. "Not the loving part. That was easy. The communicating, the honesty, the sharing part, yeah, we had to work at that. But you and Derek already do all of that."

The tightness in her throat spread to her chest. His words made sense. The feelings were easy. The rest of it was…also easy. At least with Derek.

"Open the package," Kyle said.

She looked down at the roll of paper in her lap. With some trepidation, she tore back the outer layer of wrapping.

Inside was a bunch of rhubarb.

She laughed even as she felt tears stinging her eyes.

"That's um…" Kyle said.

"Perfect," she told him. She looked up. "He knows me."

"And wants you in spite of that," Kyle said. He grinned and stood.

He had made another good point. "Tell him thanks," she said.

"You're not going to rush over to tell him yourself?"

She shook her head. "I know him too—and he needs to work at this a little."

Kyle shook his head. "Now that I've given my blessing, I can stay out of it, right?"

"That's probably safest," she agreed.

———

Her mother woke her up the next morning at six-thirty a.m. with scones. And a note from Derek saying he promised to never get scones for anyone else ever again.

The next day he delivered a yoga mat. Also at six-thirty a.m. With a note that said she was the only one he'd ever want bending over in his living room.

The next day—yep, at six-thirty—he delivered a Lindsey Stirling CD. Cracked in half.

The next, her mother awakened her to demand she go out and tell him to stop dumping little tubs of flavored creamer on their lawn. Instead, Riley took a seat on the porch swing, with a cup of black coffee, and watched him do it. She nodded politely as he declared he would never again buy flavored creamer. But when he said he'd never make coffee for another woman, she reminded him that he made coffee at the Come Again and that Scott really liked French vanilla creamer. Derek had to backtrack, and she'd gone into the house with a grin.

She did kind of like him making a big deal for her. And more, for him. He didn't work at women, and he wasn't clingy at all and it felt good to be new to him.

The morning of the path dedication and murder-mystery event, the sun was shining brightly, and she nearly tripped over the basket on the front porch when she was heading out for the town square.

The basket held a huge coffee mug and a note that said it was a *permanent* mug—not to-go and not disposable, not to be refilled and taken along, but to be used over and over again in the same kitchen. He'd also included a photo of a new mug rack on his kitchen counter with a matching mug hanging from it.

Riley felt her heart swell. That was pretty good, she had to admit. And she really wanted this to be done. She wanted to tell him how she felt. That she wanted to stay. But she was also enjoying his clinginess.

There was something she had to do first though. She dialed Lucy's number.

"Hi, Riley," her friend greeted. She sounded breathless.

"Hey, Luce. Um, so, I need to talk to you about something. I know today is busy, but could you meet me at the dedication a little early?"

"Oh, honey, I'm sorry," Lucy said. Riley heard the sound of a car driving past in the background. So Lucy was outside. "I'm behind on everything. I really can't. Can we grab a few minutes right afterward maybe? Is it really important?"

Well, it was the rest of Riley's life but... "Nah, it can wait."

"You sure? If you want to tell me over the phone, we can talk on my way to the shop."

Riley frowned. "You're running late getting to the shop?"

"Yeah."

"But, today is really huge."

"I know."

"And you never run late."

There was a pause on Lucy's end, then she said, "I know."

"Are you okay?"

Lucy laughed. "Yes. I'm okay. I had a breakfast date and it... ran longer than we expected."

Riley let all of that sink in. "You had a breakfast date? With a guy?"

"Yes, Riley, with a guy." But Lucy didn't sound irritated. She sounded...happy.

"And it 'ran long'?" Riley asked, grinning suddenly.

Lucy gave another little breathless laugh. "Yes. We got to talking and…" She sighed. Lucy actually sighed happily into the phone. "And there was some kissing."

"Oh my God, Lucy!" Riley exclaimed. "You're *dating someone*?"

"Yes! I was trying to tell you the other day when we were doing the rocks. I was going to ask you how to let Derek down. But then you got sick. And Derek finished everything up and I haven't seen much of him, so it wasn't really a pressing issue. And then we got busy with everything."

"Lucy—" Riley actually felt tears in her eyes. "I'm so happy for you."

"And I'm so happy for *you*."

"For me?"

"Your mom came into the shop yesterday to check out some books about wedding planning."

Riley groaned.

"I can't believe you let me go on and on about how sweet Derek was being to me!" Lucy said.

Riley heard a bell ring and realized Lucy had just stepped into her shop. "Well it wasn't anything sure…"

"Your mom is thrilled!"

Riley rolled her eyes. "And of course they're already planning the wedding."

Lucy laughed. "Riley, I'm so happy you're going to be around. Seriously. I've missed you."

Riley took a deep breath and let it all sink in. "Me too." And she meant it. She really did. "We have to get together soon, Luce. We have so much to talk about."

"I know! I'm dating for the *first time*! I have no idea what I'm doing!"

Riley laughed, her heart full. "We're going to talk about boys, Lucy. *Us*."

"Which means we *have* to get together and have our first official conversation on the couch in your mom's basement, right?" Lucy asked.

"I'll make cheddar popcorn *and* kettle corn."

"Deal! Okay, I'll see you at the gazebo soon."

"See you soon."

Riley hung up and took a big breath. Well, that had been easy. Just like everything else had been in Sapphire Falls. And she was beginning to think that easy was pretty damned great.

Then she headed out to the path dedication.

She'd really thought she was ready for it. But when she walked into the square, she was overwhelmed by the number of people already there. It seemed that most of the town had shown up.

Scott spotted her right away and gave her a big grin as he made a path through the crowd to her side. "Everyone's ready."

"I had no idea so many people would show," Riley said, her eyes wide.

"Oh, Hailey made sure everyone knew," he said, referring to Hailey Bennett, the Director of Business Development and Tourism for Sapphire Falls. The gorgeous, outgoing blond loved nothing more than huge crowds gathering for things in Sapphire Falls.

Riley felt a bubble of panic welling up. Hailey had thought this was worth advertising and bringing people to town? Riley had thought she'd be speaking to a small group of concerned citizens. Did these people all really understand what was going on? Had Hailey hyped this thing as something inspiring? Fun? Monumental? What was the expectation here? Her heart was racing.

Then she saw Derek.

He was on the other side of the gazebo. He stood off a bit from everyone else, but the moment he looked over and their eyes met—cheesy as it was—the tension left her. All she could really think was *I love you.*

It was bright and clear in her mind, and she felt her breath catch.

He gave her a smile, and suddenly all she wanted to do was march over there and tell him.

"Okay, showtime," Scott said.

Everyone gathered around the gazebo came back into focus and Riley shook her head. Wow. She took a deep breath. "Okay." She had to concentrate—and get this over with so she could talk to Derek.

She headed up the gazebo steps. Looking out over the crowd, she was amazed at the faces that looked back. Her parents were there. So were Derek's. Both of their grand-mothers were there, along with Hannah's. Kyle and Hannah stood with them. Scott went to join Peyton, who was grinning and almost bouncing with her excitement. She stood near her sister Hope and her husband TJ, Sapphire Falls' mayor, who was holding their little girl.

"Come here," Riley mouthed to Peyton, waving her friend forward.

Peyton shook her head.

"Yes," Riley said firmly, only then realizing that the micro-phone in front of her was on. She grinned sheepishly at the crowd and waved Peyton forward again.

Scott nudged her and she laughed, then ran up the steps to Riley's side. Riley grabbed her hand and squeezed.

Hailey was standing near the front, of course, with her husband Ty. Ty's brothers, Travis and Tucker, were with their families at the back of the crowd. There were so many Bennett kids—and *a lot* of boys—and they all looked so much alike that it was hard to tell who belonged to who as they chased and tumbled around the grass as their parents and grandparents. Kathy and Thomas, watched with big smiles.

Phoebe and Joe Spencer and their three kids were standing with Adrianne and Mason Riley, and Joe's brother and sister-in-law, Levi and Kate, and all of their kids. Levi was a multimillionaire-turned-farmer, and he'd donated the sign explaining the Peace Path, as well as making a huge donation to the Family Alliance on behalf of Sapphire Falls.

And Riley could see that all of them, every single person in that crowd, was holding a blue stone to add to the path. Suddenly she had to blink against the tears that welled up.

She barely knew Levi. She didn't know the Bennett brothers well—though she knew all their love stories. Everyone knew those stories. They had been a big deal in town. What she knew about Adrianne Riley was that she made the best cookies and muffins in four counties. She'd never had Phoebe Spencer as a teacher herself, but Mrs. Spencer had been involved in nearly everything about the school, so Riley had seen her around and spoken to her a few times. But no, she didn't really know these people that well. And yet, she felt like they were here supporting *her*. The cause too, of course, but this town...when someone here did something good, big or small, everyone backed it and supported it.

She sniffed and then chuckled when the microphone amplified the sound. At least it worked to get everyone's attention.

Which meant that when her gaze found Lucy in the crowd, standing with Bryan and Tess and Michael Kade, it took her a second to realize that Lucy was holding Kade's hand. Like holding it. Like a girlfriend would. And when Lucy met her eyes, she gave Riley a huge grin.

She took all of that in, in just a few seconds, but couldn't respond, couldn't ask any questions, couldn't actually process that Lucy was *holding hands with Michael Kade like a girlfriend would*, because Riley had to address the entire town of Sapphire Falls.

It was time.

"Hi, everyone. I'm Riley Ames," she started. "Thank you for coming. This is—" She was suddenly choked up. She had to clear her throat, and she sought Derek out in the crowd without even consciously thinking about it. He was watching her with a look of pride and love. She could see it even standing thirty feet away.

She was in the heart of the town she'd been so determined to leave, surrounded by people who had made this town a community, and more. A family. Sapphire Falls was like a big extended family. And this path was for…everyone. Victims of sex trafficking, of course, but really anyone who needed a reminder that there would always be a path home. A path to a place that was good and welcoming, where people did the right thing and made everyone who came here part of the community and, given half the chance, part of the family.

She soaked in Derek's smile, knowing that, somehow, he knew what she was thinking. And that he was feeling pretty proud of himself too. But she smiled. She wanted to be a part of this. She wanted to look across the Come Again, this town square, their backyard, and the dinner table at him for the rest of her life.

Yes, he was right. Again.

She cleared her throat, about to take the first step to truly being a part of this community.

"Thank you for coming," she started again, sounding and feeling stronger. This was just the first of many times she hoped to be standing in front of this town, talking about something awesome they'd just done. "This project is unlike anything I've *ever* done before. And I wouldn't have done it without Scott and Peyton and Lucy and Derek," she said. She didn't need to use last names here. "And my family," she added, making eye contact with her mom. "Without them believing in it, and me, it never would have happened. And I think it means something even more to me because I took a different path than this one represents. This path is about *coming* here. Finding shelter and support. My path took me *away* from Sapphire Falls. But..." She paused and took a deep breath. "Thankfully, I found my way back. And now I'm here encouraging others to walk a path that leads right to the heart of Sapphire Falls. Because this truly is a place where people can find...what they need. Maybe things they didn't even know they were looking for."

She scanned the crowd and saw Hope Bennett look up at her husband with a soft smile. Riley saw Levi Spencer put his arm around Kate and pull her close, kissing the top of her head. She watched as Tucker Bennett said something into his wife's ear that made her loop her arms around his neck and hug him hard. Riley saw Kyle and Hannah link hands. And then she looked at Derek again.

"So thank you," she said. To him and to them all. "Not just for showing up and donating, but...for being a place people can come for love, support, friendship, and family. Even if they're actually coming *back*."

Everyone clapped enthusiastically as she finished, but Riley was only interested in one reaction. And the big, hot bartender known as the Sex God actually wiped his eye.

"Peyton, do you have anything?" Riley asked, hoping to hurry it all along.

"The rocks you're holding will help complete the path," Peyton said. "But even more importantly, they are symbolic of the fact that all of us are a part of the path that leads to Sapphire Falls, for those from here, and those who find us later on." She grinned at their town. "So toss your rocks!"

Everyone cheered again as they stepped forward to line the path on either side and all tossed their blue stones onto the white and silver ones already in place. The blue filled in any gaps, and with the number of people supporting the effort, almost completely covered the white and silver.

Riley felt her eyes stinging and her heart turning over. Of course she wanted to be a part of this community. How could she not?

The crowd began dispersing, heading toward the tables for educational materials and refreshments that would lead them to Lucy's bookshop.

Riley started down the steps, needing to get to Derek.

"Riley!" Scott pulled her up short.

"Hey, can we talk la—"

"Heard you applied to the academy," he said.

"Oh, yeah."

"I'm really glad."

She smiled. "Me too."

"And I need you tonight. We have a lead on something."

Her heart thudded. She had to go with Scott, of course, but she wanted to see Derek. "Okay. I just—" She glanced around but didn't see him.

"He's on his way to the bookstore," Scott said. "I'll see you in twenty."

"Thank you!" She turned, preparing to *run* to the bookstore, but she spotted Lucy coming toward her.

Riley met her friend halfway across the space. "It was *Michael Kade* who made you late this morning by *kissing you*?" she said without preamble, pulling Lucy into a hug.

Lucy laughed. "Shhh! But yes." She was blushing prettily when she pulled back.

"That's...perfect," Riley said.

"It is." Lucy shrugged. "It all just fell into place. It was all so..."

"Easy," Riley filled in.

Lucy nodded. "Yeah."

"Well," Riley said. "They do call it *falling* in love. Falling is easy. You just let yourself go and it happens."

Lucy grinned. "Yes. Exactly."

"And now, I need to go. To your bookshop. To tell a man I love him."

"Go!"

And she did. She ran all the way to the shop.

Riley caught Derek just as his hand reached for the bookshop door.

"Hey."

He turned. "Hey."

"I love you."

He dropped his hand and turned to face her fully. But he said nothing.

"Did you hear me?" she asked.

"Well, yeah." He arched a brow. "I was waiting for more."

She propped a hand on her hip. "More? Like what?"

He shrugged. "Something *else*. I already knew that part."

Her heart warmed. "Oh."

He grinned. "How about you tell me that this little tantrum of yours is over."

She frowned. "Tantrum? Really? Being sure that you really do feel the way you say you feel? Making you *work* at winning a woman over? Making you—"

"See? Your cheeks are pink and your voice is rising," he broke in. "Tantrum."

She realized he was pushing her buttons. As usual. "If you're not going to take me seriously and you're going to argue with *everything*, then I don't know about this after all."

"But you love me."

She felt a little thrill shoot through her. "Yeah, but I also kind of want to smother you with a pillow."

His grin grew. "So that's a yes to the question about whether you'll be back in my bed tonight."

She fought her smile. "You might want to sleep with an eye open."

"Oh, I don't intend to do a lot of sleeping at all."

And just like that, heat and desire swept through her. And happiness. There was a huge dose of that too. "I have to work tonight. I don't know when I'll be done."

He shrugged and took a step toward her. "Well, I'm doing these crazy cemetery tours, so I'll be late too. Come over whenever."

"Oh, that reminds me..." She rummaged in her bag and pulled out the black T-shirt she'd bought him. "I need you to wear this tonight while you do the tours."

He caught it when she tossed it to him. He shook it out and held it up and read, "*I licked it so it's mine.*" He grinned. "I like it."

"It will keep your tour groupies away."

He slung it over his shoulder. "That's kind of clingy of you."

She nodded. "Yep. Get used to it."

He stepped closer. "I think I'll manage."

She sighed heavily. "Well, fair warning—I think it might get even worse. I might want to marry you eventually."

"Wow, that's pretty cliché," he said, but his eyes were swirling with emotion.

"I think I'll manage," she said, echoing his statement.

He was nearly on top of her now. "Well, tell you what. We won't be totally traditional Sapphire Falls. We'll work past midnight every night and sleep late every day and we'll make a living hacking bad guys and making pizza."

"Oh *yes*." She wrapped her arms around his neck. "Let's stay up late and sleep late for sure. I guess until we have kids at least."

His eyes got hot and possessive. "We could homeschool."

"Now *that* would make my mom crazy," Riley said. "Let's totally do that."

Derek put his hands on her ass. "She'll really just be glad you're here, you know."

Riley nodded. "Yeah. Most of the time."

"And I can help with those other times."

Her heart softened and she rose onto her tiptoes. "You *are* really good at *handling* me."

"Yeah, I am." He squeezed her ass and leaned in. "And don't think for one second that's *easy*." Then he kissed her hot and hard.

When he finally lifted his head, she sighed happily. "Okay, let's go do our night owl thing and I'll meet you at home later." Man, she really loved calling his place *home*.

"Sounds perfect." He kissed her again and then let her go.

She turned and started down the sidewalk.

"And, Ry?"

She looked back. "Yeah?"

"I love you too."

She gave him a big smile. "I know."

He winked. "So, bring your mug. The big heavy ceramic one that's just a lot easier to keep at my place and use there every morning. Forever."

Feeling her heart nearly overflowing, she nodded. "You know...you're pretty good at this clingy stuff too."

"Yep. Get used to it."

She already was.

———

Thank you for reading *Getting All Riled Up*! I hope you loved Derek and Riley!

Don't miss the big Sapphire Falls wedding in **Getting to the Church On Time**!

The wedding of the year will be absolutely perfect...
Except for the massive snowstorm about to hit town.

But Sapphire Falls always looks on the bright side. And they don't cancel a perfectly good party, even for Jack Frost.

There will be a wedding… the only question is who will be walking down the aisle?

Grab **Getting to the Church On Time** now!

————

The Sapphire Falls series

Getting Out of Hand
Getting Worked Up
Getting Dirty
Getting Wrapped Up
Getting It All
Getting Lucky
Getting Over It
Getting His Way
Getting Into Trouble
Getting It Right
Getting All Riled Up
Getting to the Church On Time

And more at
ErinNicholas.com

————

Join in on the fan fun too! I love interacting with my readers and would love to have you in the two places where I chat with fans the most--my email list and my Super Fan page on Facebook!

Sign up for my email list! You'll hear from me just a couple times a month and I'll keep you updated on all my news, sales, exclusive fun, and new releases!
http://bit.ly/ErinNicholasEmails

Join my fan page on Facebook at Erin Nicholas Super Fans! I check in there every day and it's the best place for first looks, exclusive giveaways, book talk and fun!

ABOUT ERIN

Erin Nicholas is the New York Times and USA Today bestselling author of over thirty sexy contemporary romances. Her stories have been described as toe-curling, enchanting, steamy and fun. She loves to write about reluctant heroes, imperfect heroines and happily ever afters. She lives in the Midwest with her husband who only wants to read the sex scenes in her books, her kids who will never read the sex scenes in her books, and family and friends who say they're shocked by the sex scenes in her books (yeah, right!).

Find her and all her books at
www.ErinNicholas.com

And find her on Facebook, BookBub, and Instagram!

9 780998 894713